Out of the Rain

**Also by Elizabeth Cadell
In Thorndike Large Print:**

THE CUCKOO IN SPRING
THE GOLDEN COLLAR
HONEY FOR TEA

Out of the Rain

Elizabeth Cadell

THORNDIKE PRESS • THORNDIKE, MAINE

Library of Congress Cataloging-in-Publication Data

Cadell, Elizabeth.
   Out of the rain.

      "Thorndike large print"—T.p. verso.
      1. Large type books.   I. Title
   [PR6005.A22509   1988]   823'.914   88-2146
   ISBN 0-89621-148-7 (lg. print: alk. paper)

Large Print edition available in North America by arrangement
with William Morrow & Company, Inc., New York.

Cover design by Bernie Beckman.

Out of the Rain

1

The meeting was to be at three thirty. It was now close on one o'clock and Edward Netherford, leaving his office and directing his steps to the restaurant at which he usually lunched, found his appetite diminishing at the thought of what the afternoon was to bring.

Three clients. No lawyer could prosper without clients, but he had seen something of these three when his father—now deceased—had dealt with them, and the thought of meeting them again gave him a feeling of distaste.

It would be sensible, he decided, taking his place at a corner table and waving aside the proffered menu, to put work out of his mind and enjoy his avocado and grilled sole. It was absurd to wish that his secretary, Miss Cave, could have been present at this afternoon's meeting to perform her customary task of quelling aggressive clients. She had done this for the thirty years during which she had been his father's secretary—but she was at this moment enjoying her annual holiday up at Inverness. She never varied her programme: the first three weeks of June; up to Fort William by night sleeper; by boat along the Caledonian canal to Inverness to visit her widowed sister. Edward was always relieved at her departure, for since his father's death, she had transferred her loyalty and efficiency to himself, but she had unfortunately retained the faintly patronising, kind-but-firm nurse's manner in which she had treated him since he joined the firm at the age of twenty-five. Now he was thirty-three, and a junior partner and he felt that the time for nursing was past. Only on occasions like this, when he had to face three arrogant and bullying clients, did he miss her talent for putting people in their place.

He finished his coffee, signed the bill, glanced out at the June sunshine and decided to walk back to the office through the Park. He went slowly, looking at the flowers and the deck chairs and the groups of young people seated on the grass. Not a day to be spent in London, he thought. A day for the open countryside, for old farmhouses and grazing cows and clucking hens. He had never been able to understand how his father, born and bred in

Somerset, could have been content with a working life spent in London, with only brief visits to the cottage he had kept when he sold his estate.

A lovely day. But not for him. For him, an office on the third floor of a high-rise block, rooms neatly labelled with the names of their occupants, carpeted corridors and a room overlooking a busy thoroughfare. An imposing desk, a swivel chair, bookshelves, a sofa and comfortable chairs for clients. A small anteroom containing filing cabinets, a hat stand, a door to a small but well-fitted shower room. If he sometimes thought of this as a cage, he acknowledged that it was a pleasant one. And neat—as neat as the three rooms he occupied in a block of flats in Chiswick. A service flat, they called it, and the service was good. Breakfast brought to him each morning, staff to clean up when he was out. Not spacious, but a place for everything and everything in its place—a habit he had acquired during his school days and had never lost. A bachelor set-up. And escape, when he needed it, to his father's old cottage in Somerset.

He was at his desk. Three twenty. He opened the file that had been placed ready for his perusal.

Here it all was. William Brockman, deceased. His Will, drawn up by Edward's father. Letters—mostly of complaint; William Brockman had always demanded his money's worth. An odd business, Edward reflected, his marriage to the housekeeper. On the one hand, a titled wife and three children. On the other hand . . . bit of a shock for the children, all of middle age, to have had to swallow that second ménage. They must have—

His thoughts were interrupted by a discreet knock on the door. Miss Cave's assistant appeared. She was new to the job. Miss Cave's assistants never stayed long. But this one looked tougher than her predecessors; perhaps she would be able to stand up to the Cave-woman.

"Some clients to see you, Mr. Netherford. Mr. Roger Brockman, Miss Millicent Brockman and Miss Audrey Brockman."

"Show them in, please."

With their entrance, the spacious office seemed to shrink. Edward thought he had never seen more massive women. Their brother, of average height and weight, looked, by contrast, a bantam. When they had been invited to seat themselves, their voices proved to match their appearance. Millicent boomed, Audrey trumpeted. Roger's voice was hoarse—

the result, Edward supposed, of a lifetime spent in trying to make himself heard. He began to address Edward, but did not get far.

"I suppose you know all the facts of this case. We—"

"Of course he knows the facts," broke in Audrey. "He was sent a letter setting them out quite clearly."

"And he knows, or should know, the details of our previous dealings with this firm," Millicent added.

Roger was looking round the office, apparently making comparisons with his last visit.

"You haven't changed this room at all," he observed. "Since your father died, I mean. Except that his portrait's on the wall."

Millicent gave him a malevolent glance.

"Will you kindly keep your attention on what's going on?" she asked him.

In spite of the warmth of the weather, all three were wearing heavy tweed suits. Audrey's was a heather mixture, Millicent's a too-large checked design. Roger's was grey. They looked more than their age, Edward thought—or perhaps it was their self-assurance that added some years to their fifty-or-so. They looked, and were, a prosperous trio.

"I propose," Audrey pronounced, "to begin

11

at the beginning."

Edward murmured that this would be wise.

"Your father," she proceeded, "drew up my father's—our father's—Will."

"That is so."

"There was no hitch of any kind."

"None, as far as I can see from the files."

"My father was a widower when the Will was drawn up. He left everything to his children—my sister and my brother and myself."

Edward nodded. Millicent took up the tale.

"When my sister said that everything had been left to us," she said, "she left out a most important fact. My mother owned three pictures—three Impressionist pictures—which on her death she left to my father for his lifetime. On his death, they were to pass to the three of us. The three pictures were specifically mentioned in the Will—you must have a copy of it there."

"I have."

"Then you know that we have a legal right to them. My father died at the beginning of last year. He—"

"Tenth of March, to be exact," Roger said.

"And since then—"

"Will you please not interrupt?" Millicent snapped at him. "I was about to tell Mr.

Netherford about the discovery we made after my mother's death."

Edward waited.

"A shocking revelation," Audrey intoned. "My father had been conducting an affair with our housekeeper. Even during my mother's lifetime we had suspected that this . . . . this liaison had been going on."

"In our house, in our *own house*," Millicent said on a sepulchral note. "We had our suspicions, but my father had never been a philanderer. It all came out when my mother died. Soon afterwards my father went away with the housekeeper."

"They went back to where she had come from—Yorkshire," said Roger.

"How long ago was that, exactly?" Edward asked.

"Matter of four years. He married her and he lived in her house until he died."

"And since he died," Audrey said, "we've been trying to get our pictures out of his widow."

"And haven't succeeded," said Millicent. "That's why we've come to you."

"The pictures," Roger filled in, "aren't Monets or Manets. They wouldn't fetch astronomical prices at Christie's or Sotheby's. But they're genuine Impressionists and by my reckoning, by present-day values, they'd fetch at least twenty thousand pounds apiece. That's a good sum. I don't say we'd want to sell them, but they're ours and we want to get them away from that woman. But she's hanging on. We want you to make her give them up."

"And what I want to know," Audrey said, "is how you propose to set about it."

Edward surveyed them, hoping his intense dislike was not written on his face. He thought them smug and snobbish. The contemptuous manner in which Audrey had uttered the word housekeeper said much for the outworn social standards of the trio.

She was speaking again.

"When my mother died and my father's double life was discovered, he went with his mistress, as I told you, to live in Yorkshire. He handed over to the three of us his capital and the furniture and effects, but not the pictures. He took the pictures to Yorkshire with him. Since he died, the three of us, the executors of the estate, have been trying to get them out of his widow. Without success."

"What steps have you taken?" Edward asked.

"The usual," Roger replied. "We attended my father's funeral in York. She was at the cemetery, but she was surrounded by a group

14

of what we took to be her relations, and it was clear that she was avoiding us. Before any of us could get a word with her, she drove away. So we returned to London and wrote her a letter asking her to make arrangements to forward our pictures to our London address."

"No reply," said Audrey.

"Not a line," said Millicent. "So we wrote by registered post."

"Still no reply," said Audrey.

"We then copied out the part of the Will relating to the pictures, and sent it to her—again by registered post."

"Not a word in reply," said Audrey. "So we decided to go up and see her. We drove up to York. When we called at her house, which is near the Minster, she didn't answer the door. She was obviously watching from a window. In fact, we caught a glimpse of her behind the curtains. We went back and tried again the next day."

"Then," said Millicent, "we realised that it was useless, and returned to London. And that's where the matter stands now."

"We wrote—again by registered post," Roger said, "to inform her that we were putting the matter into the hands of a lawyer."

"You," said Audrey, and fixed her small, cold eyes on Edward.

There was a pause.

"Have you considered the possibility," Edward asked, "that she has sold the pictures?"

"Yes," Millicent answered, "we have. But although they are not, as we've said before, well known, I think it likely—or my brother thinks it likely—that there would have been some kind of notice, or comment, if they had been put on the market. What seems clear to me is that if she's hanging on to them—as she is—she must intend to sell them eventually."

"And so," Audrey said, "some action must be taken to prevent her. What steps are you going to take?"

Edward was tired of their hectoring tone and bullying manner. The paintings, which he had never seen, held little interest for him. His father had thought them good and had on more than one occasion expressed the opinion that they were undervalued, but to Edward they were merely the cause of the present wrangle. A nuisance to one and all.

"I shall take the usual steps," he told them. "I shall see if she answers my correspondence. If she doesn't, it may come to a court order. She may find dealing with the law a different proposition to ignoring your letters." He paused. "What sort of woman is she?"

"A harpy," said Audrey unhesitatingly.

"As cunning as they come," Roger added. "Look at the way she lived in our house carrying on this affair with my father."

"How old is she?" Edward asked.

"In her early fifties," Millicent answered. "She's short and stout and quite plain, and talks with a Yorkshire accent. What my father saw in her, I can't imagine."

Edward felt that there was no point in prolonging the interview. After a few final words, he rang for Miss Cave's assistant and had the clients shown out. Then he gave a sign of relief and reflected with pleasure that he could now await the return of Miss Cave and place the matter in her hands. All he needed to do in the interval was to advise the second Mrs. Brockman that he was in charge of the case and would be glad to know what steps she was taking to deliver the three pictures to their owners.

He wrote to her. He did not expect a reply, and did not get one. The next move, he thought with relief, was up to Miss Cave.

But Miss Cave, returning and gathering up the reins, was not pleased with his conduct of the case.

"Just like your father," she said, "He took a great dislike to all the Brockmans, and was only anxious to get the Will drawn up so that

17

he could forget the family. I could never understand what he had against them. They're no worse than many of our other clients."

"I doubt that," Edward said.

"They're the bullying type, I grant you that. But they're only what their upbringing made them. Their mother was an out-and-out snob. Their father was rather a nice man, and although I don't approve of his liaison with the housekeeper, I'm glad he found some escape from his wife and three stuck-up children."

"Did you ever see the three pictures?"

"Yes. They were shown to your father and to me when we visited the house to check some items of an inventory. If you'd told me they were Renoirs, I wouldn't have contradicted you. Did they gather what they're worth today?"

"Roger Brockman thought they'd fetch about twenty thousand pounds apiece."

"For genuine Impressionists? He must know that's nonsense."

"Perhaps. If his figure is too low, perhaps the housekeeper has had them valued and—"

"—decided to keep them? Well, it's your job to see that she doesn't."

She spoke irritably. She invariably returned from her holiday in a bad mood. Evidently the air of Inverness did not suit her.

He was able to forget the Brockmans for two weeks. Then Miss Cave came to him with a newly opened file, placed it on his desk and spoke with decision.

"You've got to go up there," she said.

He looked at her with a frown.

"Go up? Go up where?"

"You've got to go up to Yorkshire and see that woman—Mrs. Brockman. We're not getting anywhere through the post."

"What makes you think—"

"—that your going up will produce results? She'll let you in, for a start. She's got nothing against you. She probably loathes the trio of Brockmans—and probably with good cause. She must have put up with a lot from them during her years in their service. All she's doing now is getting some of her own back. When you get up there, you'll probably find her open to reason."

"Why should *I* be the one to go? There are others in the firm that I could send."

"Mrs. Brockman isn't in a mood to deal with underlings. She'll only treat with a principal of Netherford and Netherford. You'll enjoy the trip—I presume you'll be driving?"

"If I go, I shall certainly drive."

"This is the best time of year to see the Yorkshire moors," she reminded him by way of consolation. "Don't fix a definite return date—you can't tell how long you'll need. I'll book you into Mr. Parton's hotel."

He made no reply. Miss Cave's decisions were not reached lightly, and had seldom been questioned. He would have to go up to Yorkshire. He would have to call on a troublesome woman and hope that Miss Cave's forecast of her cooperation would prove a correct one.

There was not much preparation to make on the domestic front. He had only to tell the staff at his flat that he would be away for a short while. Everything would be taken care of. He would return to find his linen cleaned and put away. His refrigerator would be replenished, his rooms tidied. He would leave, and return to the neatness and order which had become part of his existence.

He made one or two telephone calls to cancel engagements he had made with friends—but he was not a man who had many social commitments. His circle was restricted to the few people who had been able to break through the barrier of shyness behind which he was imprisoned, and reach the pleasant, mildly humorous man beyond. He had struggled all his life to overcome this disability—without success. The picture he presented to the world was one of seriousness bordering on solemnity—a stiffness of manner that made him seem older than his years. With only a few friends could he relax. One of these was Tom Parton, who owned a hotel near York and with whom he would soon be recalling memories of their schooldays together. If this journey to the north had any compensations, it was the opportunity of seeing Tom again.

2

The four days before his departure were fine and sunny. He played some golf, got a few games of tennis and found himself getting sunburnt. But on the day he was to leave London, the good weather turned sour. He hoped it would improve before his return.

The drive began in pleasant conditions. The sky was overcast, but there was no rain. It was only when he reached the Doncaster bypass that there appeared to be a worsening of the weather. The sky seemed to be coming lower. The light faded, and he found himself driving in semi-darkness. Then the rain began to fall. When he stopped shortly afterwards for petrol, the driver of a car beside his called a question.

"Going far?"

"York."

The man looked up at the ever-increasing rain.

"I'm glad I'm heading south. You're going to catch it, you are. Looks like you're running straight into it."

Edward found this forecast only too accurate. The rain, beginning as a drizzle, became a downpour. He could hear distant peals of thunder; lightning flashed through the thickening mist.

When he had driven some distance with water streaming down his windscreen, he decided to halt for a while to give the storm a chance of abating. He stopped at the next roadhouse—one that on a fine evening no doubt looked inviting with bright lights and illuminated sign, but which when he came to it now was shrouded in mist. He parked his car, held his anorak over his head and hurried inside. Here, except for the rumbling of thunder, there was comfort and good cheer. At the bar were groups of travellers who, like himself, had come in for shelter.

He decided to dine in the restaurant. Tom Parton's hotel, to which he was bound, was famous not only for its history and antiquity, but also for its cuisine, but he had set out too late to dine there.

The restaurant was full, most of the tables being occupied by clergymen on their way, he guessed, to one of the frequent clerical gatherings held in York. He was not alone at this table, but the man with whom he had to share proved an agreeable companion.

"I suppose June is the time for thunderstorms," he remarked as the menus were placed before them. "But this is going too far. Are you going north or south?"

"North."

"Then you're unlucky. I'm going south, away from it. How far are you going?"

"Just beyond York."

"Nice city. I had a job once—long ago—taking tourists round it. It's a place you never get tired of. I suppose you know it?"

"Fairly well."

"Staying with friends?"

"No. I'm going to a hotel called the Cross Keys."

"Is that so? I know it well. Small but well run."

"It's run, as a matter of fact, by an old schoolfriend of mine—Tom Parton."

"He took over from his father, didn't he?"

"And grandfather. And greatgrandfather. They've had the place for two hundred years." He studied the menu. "Shrimp and then steak, I think," he told the waiter.

He and his companion shared a half bottle of wine between them.

"No danger of being had up for driving offences on a night like this," remarked the stranger. "I was only doing fifteen miles an hour for the last part of the journey."

Over his coffee in the lounge, Edward thought the rain was less heavy than it had been on his arrival. He might, he thought, have given it a little more time, but he was anxious to get on. It was already eight forty, Tom's hotel was on the farther side of York, and travelling would be slow. He paid his bill and was accompanied to his car by a hall porter holding open a giant-size umbrella.

Rain, he thought as he went on his way, was all very well to keep the garden plants happy, but this kind of downpour made him feel like a denizen of a tropical forest. More thunder and lightning, a brief lull and then a renewed cascade.

It was almost ten o'clock when he drove through York and took the road to the village of Balderwick. Soon he was in open country. Ahead was the hotel, and shelter and comfort.

Ahead was also a bright glow which might, he thought, be the lights of a town—if there had been a town in that direction. But York was off to the left—and the glow was on the right.

He got nearer, and suspicion became certainty. Something was on fire. Certainty was followed by apprehension. If it wasn't the Cross Keys, it was very near it.

It was the Cross Keys. As he drew up behind the line of fire engines and cars and the sea of umbrellas belonging to the sightseers who had gathered, he saw that the blaze had been brought under control—but part of the building was still smouldering.

He put on his anorak, pulled the hood over his head and stepped out into the driving rain. Making his way through the watchers, he looked for and found the proprietor of the hotel, his face smoke-blackened, his voice hoarse.

"My God, Tom." Edward spoke in a shocked voice. "What caused it?"

"Hello, Edward. No room at the Inn tonight, I'm afraid. It was lightning that did it. A bang like several bombs going off—and then the roof caught fire. The fire engines arrived in time to save most of the building. I've got to go. Will you fix yourself up for the night? I sent all the guests to the Apex hotel in York. There'll be accommodation for you there. Can't stop—sorry."

He was gone. After watching the scene for some time, Edward felt rain trickling down

26

into his shirt, and turned away. He could do nothing by staying.

It was not a long drive—eight miles—to York and the Apex hotel. Going in and asking for a room, he met with a firm negative. The hotel, said the reception clerk, was full to overflowing. It had been full of clergymen, but the arrival of the refugees from the Cross Keys had created a crisis. Those of them who could not be accommodated had been redirected to other hotels.

"We're sorry, sir." The clerk spoke in a voice of exhaustion. "We've had crowds milling round the hall and the lounges, demanding rooms. The telephone hasn't stopped ringing. Our staff can't do any more. But we've made lists of hotels and boarding houses that you could try." He turned to a colleague. "Hand me one of those papers, will you, Dave."

The list was a typed one. Hotels were at the top of the page, boarding houses next, and bed and breakfast accommodation last of all.

"Hope you get fixed up, sir," the clerk said. "There's not only clergymen. There's another lot calling themselves the Apostles of Melody."

"Pop group?" Edward enquired.

27

"No, sir. Classical. They meet twice a year, but they've never chosen York before."

Edward went out to his car and sat studying the list. He'd better get started, he told himself. Getting on for eleven. He thought it best, in view of the crowded conditions in the city, to go straight down the list. It was no use being choosey at this stage.

It was past eleven when he had worked through the hotels and half the boarding houses. It had been a swift operation—out of the car, into the establishment, instant refusals, polite or not-so-polite. It was still raining.

He did not try the bed and breakfast places. At the last boarding house, he heard the refusal and confronted the shirt-sleeved proprietor and his wife.

"Do you know of any place that's not on the list?" he asked them.

"Why don't you try the bed and breakfasts?" enquired the woman.

"I will if I have to, but—"

"The only place I know of," said the man, "is bed and breakfast—it's on the list, but it—"

"If you're talking about Pantiles, it's not on offer any more," said the woman.

"You sure about that?" demanded her husband.

"Certain. But he could try. It's a bit off the main road and you might have difficulty in finding it," she told Edward, "but there might be this room vacant. It's a nice house. Far as I remember, the offer was for only one guest. Want to try?"

Edward decided that he had no choice. It was either this bed and breakfast, which sounded possible, or the others on the list, which he felt looked uninviting.

He found himself back on the road leading to Balderwick. The glow of the fire was still visible. Round him were fields—sodden, he guessed, after this rain. He passed no signpost until he was about four miles from York—then he saw through the mist a low wooden arrow. On it was painted a name: Pantiles.

The car clock said half past eleven. Was there any hope, he wondered, of getting into a house—a respectable house—at this hour? It would probably be in darkness, closed and shuttered.

And then, ahead and a little to the right, he discerned a light. He drove up to it and found himself brought to a halt by a three-barred gate. It was partly open; by edging the car gently forward, inch by inch, he managed to drive through it. He stopped before the lighted door and got out of the car.

The light enabled him to see a glass-enclosed portico in which was a large pram, three folded deck chairs and a plant in a wicker basket suspended from the ceiling. The door on the farther side was closed. He could see neither bell nor knocker. He rapped on a pane of glass, wondering as he did so if the inmates of the house would venture to open the door at this late hour.

He had to knock again. He could hear inside the house a sound almost as loud as the thudding of the rain. Then the door opened, and he recognised the sound: it was the howling of a baby.

In the doorway stood a tall girl with an infant resting against her shoulder. The infant, clearly displeased with life, was giving forth yells of such volume that Edward could scarcely believe his ears—so small a voice box, so loud a voice.

The girl's lips moved, but Edward could not hear what she was saying. A woman behind her moved forward and motioned him inside. Avoiding the low-hanging plant, he entered. The baby, seeing him, suspended its howls.

"I'm sorry to arrive at this hour," Edward said, "but I'm more or less stranded."

As briefly as he could, he outlined his

efforts to find accommodation.

"Who on earth sent you here?" asked the girl in surprise.

She must be in her middle twenties, Edward thought. A well-made girl, dressed in jeans and a coloured shirt. Hair shoulder-length and unbrushed. Wedding ring. The woman beside her was shorter, older, and had once been very pretty. She was wearing an ankle-length robe of pale pink and there was a silk band round her hair.

"It was someone in the last boarding house I called at. Is it correct that you're offering bed and breakfast?"

"Yes and no," said the girl.

"We did once, some time ago," the older woman added. "Nobody came."

Perhaps somebody had come, Edward thought, heard the howls and gone away again.

They closed the door behind him and led him through a wide hall from which opened a combined dining and drawing room which his brief glance told him looked both untidy and unlived-in. Then they were in a large and obviously lived-in kitchen. In the centre was a table round which were ranged four tall-backed pinewood chairs. In a corner was a small, low, square table—like the larger table, plastic-topped—at which were placed two small chairs and an infant's high chair. Through the glass panels of a door facing him he could see an exceptionally well-equipped utility room—a washing machine, a dishwasher, a refrigerator, a tall deepfreezer. Both rooms had double stainless sinks.

The girl addressed Edward.

"Take off that anorak—it's dripping," she directed. He handed it to her and she draped it on the back of a chair. "My names's Estelle Denby. This is my mother, Mrs. Mallin."

Edward acknowledged the introduction, gave his name and added that he was a lawyer who had come up to York on business.

As he was speaking, an elderly man came into the room. He looked about seventy, tall and thin and stooping, with sparse grey hair. He looked with mild enquiry at Edward.

"My father," Mrs. Mallin told him. "Mr. Mundy. This is Mr. Netherford, Father. Someone sent him here and told him we might be able to give him a bed and breakfast."

"Extraordinary," murmured Mr. Mundy. "Really extraordinary." His voice was pleasant, his manner friendly. "Who would have thought that this house would still have been on the list? It must be—how long, Celia?—since we put our names on it."

"Best part of two years," said Mrs. Mallin.

"We can give you a room for the night and we can give you breakfast," Estelle said. "But I'm not a professional at the job, so you might care to go off after breakfast and fix yourself up somewhere else."

"You'll find accommodation hard to get—as you've already discovered," Mrs. Mallin said. "The place is full of clergymen, and besides there's a group called . . . I forget what."

"The Apostles of Melody," Edward supplied.

"A very rum lot," said Mr. Mundy.

A mixed choir, Edward thought—the grandfather's voice low and muted, the mother's brisk and middle-register, the girl's rather high and very clear, with something in it that suggested she found life amusing.

The baby, perhaps feeling himself neglected, set up another howl. Estelle rubbed her cheek gently against his downy head, and rocked gently to and fro. Then he stopped, his eyes on the door. Two small figures were standing regarding Edward with lively curiosity.

"Darlings, *bed*," Estelle said firmly.

"It's our fault for taking them out to see the fire," Mr. Mundy said. "They're wide awake now."

"I stopped there to talk to the owner, who's a friend of mine," Edward said.

33

"Tom Parton. You know him?" Estelle asked in surprise.

"We were at school together."

"He's our greatest friend. That's why we took the children to see the fire."

It seemed to Edward an odd entertainment for toddlers, but he did not say so. Estelle, still cradling the baby, was shepherding the two small boys out of the room.

"The older one's called Hugo," she told Edward. "The smaller one's Maurice. The baby's called Damien. Off you go, you two. *Bed*. In fact, off we all go," she went on. "We're usually in bed at this hour. If it hadn't been for the fire, you wouldn't have found us up."

"How did you know I wasn't an intruder?"

"Intruders don't usually drive up to the front door with headlights full on. Mother, will you show Mr. Netherford to his room? When the bed and breakfast idea folded," she told Edward, "we turned the room into a playroom for the children. I hope you'll find your way through the toys."

"I'll bring in my suitcase." Edward put his anorak over his head, went out in the still-pouring rain to the car and returned with his luggage. He said goodnight to Estelle and Mr. Mundy and then followed Mrs. Mallin along

34

a corridor. She opened a door and switched on a light, revealing a room in which was a bed, a chair, a cupboard, a small bedside table and a varied assortment of children's toys.

"If you'll move some of those toys out of the way," she said, "I'll make up the bed."

She went out and returned with a counterpane and a matching sheet. She put fresh covers on the pillows, and while she worked, Edward made a pathway through the scattered toys, most of which were woolly animals in a grievous state of disrepair. He observed with relief that the room had its own bathroom.

"There you are." Mrs. Mallin patted the pillows."You ought to sleep well—the bed's comfortable. The children usually come in here first thing in the morning, but we'll keep them away tomorrow. Anything else you want?"

"No, thank you."

Closing the door behind her, he swung his suitcase on to the chair and took out the things he would need for the night. Going into the bathroom, he swerved to avoid another hanging plant. People of average height, he mused resentfully, could dodge them—but he was of more than average height, and he disliked having his hair disarranged by greenery.

He removed several small plastic animals

that were floating in the washbasin, washed, cleaned his teeth and then got into bed. It was as comfortable as Mrs. Mallin had said it was. He slept heavily, and woke later than usual—eight thirty to his normal seven thirty. He lay with his eyes on the wide window, slowly registering the fact that it was a sunny, windless day. Birds were singing loudly. He rose and threaded his way between an assortment of miniature farm animals, and stood at the window making a survey.

There was no other building in sight. The house, one-storied, was set in the middle of a large field surrounded by trees and a low stone wall. He could see the narrow road and the three-barred gate through which he had entered last night. There was no garden, no flower beds. The only sign of cultivation was an area on which grew neat rows of vegetables. This was surrounded by a mesh screen—to keep out the children, he guessed. A small structure, not much larger than a summer-house—perhaps the cottage of the non-existent gardener—stood in a far corner. Far off, he could see rising from wooded areas tall chimneys. An odd situation, he thought. The house, or bungalow, or cottage—he was undecided what to name it—looked as though it had been built elsewhere and then transported here and parked in the middle of the field.

The most pleasant—he almost called it the only redeeming—feature of the landscape was a narrow, sun-flecked river—hardly more than a stream—that flowed slowly from a hidden point among some trees, and made a wide loop before disappearing into the distance. Along its banks were willows which seemed to offer shady stopping-places for strollers or picnickers. He could see moorhens and a stately swan. He turned from the window remembering that he, too, could look from his rooms onto flowing water.

He had a bath, dressed and as a gesture of hope packed his suitcase; he would go round a few hotels and find out if by chance a room was now vacant. He had slept comfortably enough last night, but a longer stay with babies did not attract him. Domesticity and family life were all very well, but they were not for him—not, at any rate, for the present.

He went out of the bedroom and walked along the corridor to the kitchen door. There was not a sound in the house. All asleep? he wondered. But his limited knowledge of babies told him that they were usually up at dawn, clamouring for food or attention.

He was learning something about the set-up, he thought. Biggish house, all on one floor. Mother, who seemed to be a mixture of briskness and vagueness. Grandfather, who seemed a decent fellow. And the girl, who must have her hands full with three babies to see to. He wondered where her husband was.

There was nobody in the dining-drawing room, but the table was laid with a blue checked cloth, a plate, a knife and fork and spoon and a cup and saucer. Laid for his breakfast, he surmised. He discovered that he was very hungry—but although it was close on half past nine, there was no smell of coffee, no sound of bacon sizzling in the pan, no toast rack ready to receive evenly-cut slices of toast. He always enjoyed his breakfast, and always had a substantial one—an egg fried on toast, accompanied by a couple of tomatoes in season, preceded by a cereal and followed by more toast and two aromatic cups of coffee. So much had he come to take this service for granted, that its absence gave him a hollow feeling.

He went into the kitchen. Seated by a sunny window was Mrs. Mallin, placidly working at a length of knitting. She looked up and wished him good morning, and asked if he had slept well.

"Very well, thank you."

She nodded and went on with her work.

She was in a green linen skirt with a jersey in a paler colour. Her hair was drawn into a neat coil.

The silence lengthened. After some minutes, Edward asked if her daughter and the children were in the house.

"No. Never at this time," she said. She paused to count a row of stitches. "This is a very comfortable house, but it's in a rather inconvenient place. No deliveries. Everything has to be fetched: bread, milk, groceries, newspapers, everything. My daughter goes out every morning in the car with the three children, summer or winter, and brings back the day's supplies. In that way, she can give the babies an outing and leave herself free to do the housework during the rest of the morning. Today, my father went with her—he needed some seeds for his vegetable garden."

The housework, Edward thought, looking round him, did not seem to come in for much attention. There was unwashed crockery in the sink, toys everywhere, a wide variety of baby food spread on the table, and an assortment of stores in jars on the working counters.

"Perhaps," he suggested, "I could help by getting my own breakfast."

"Oh, don't worry," Mrs. Mallin answered. "Estelle will be back soon." She glanced at the wall clock. "In fact, she's slightly late. You could go and wait for the car. There's always a lot to take out of it."

He went to the front door and opened it. Across the field he could see approaching a small, extremely shabby car. It stopped outside the front door. Estelle was at the wheel. Beside her was Mr. Mundy and behind were the three children, the baby in a travelling cot. Mr. Mundy descended, lifted out the two small boys and then reached in for the baby's cot. This he carried inside, wishing Edward good morning on the way.

"Lovely day," Estelle called.

Said like that, it sounded a lovely day. There was something in her voice which with some reluctance he labelled a lilt. But he was in no condition to appreciate lilts; his stomach was making sounds of deprivation.

He helped Estelle and her grandfather to unload the stores. These were carried into the kitchen and deposited in any available clear space; then Edward waited hopefully for promises of an immediate breakfast.

"Hungry?" enquired Estelle.

"Well yes, I am, rather."

"Toast and coffee, or the whole works?"

"Egg and bacon, if that's all right."

She looked neat and fresh and sun-tanned.

She lifted the baby boy from the cot and handed it to Mrs. Mallin, who put aside her knitting needles and held him on her lap.

"The tooth's through," Estelle told Edward with satisfaction. "I'm sorry he yelled last night." She turned from the cupboard in which she had been putting away stores. "The other two produced their teeth without a squeak—no trouble at all." She held up a plastic bag. "Look—lovely fresh bread. I buy it every morning." She drew the two small boys towards her and peeled off their jerseys. "Now it's warmer you can go and play in the garden," she told them. "Grandad will put on your wellies."

"Tricycle?" enquired Hugo.

"No—the fields will be too wet for tricycles. Don't worry Grandad; he's got seeds to plant. Now off you go. Mr. Netherford wants his breakfast."

"Is this man Mr. Netherford?"

"This gentleman is Mr. Netherford, yes."

"Did he sleep here?"

"He slept here. Now he's awake and he wants his breakfast, so don't stay talking."

"I'll come back later on," Hugo said, and shepherded his brother out of doors.

"He talks very well," Edward remarked. "How old is he?"

"Three and a half, but he's been a conversationalist since he was two. It was talking to my grandfather that started him off," explained Estelle. "I used to leave his pram next to the vegetable patch and the two of them prattled non-stop. Maurice talks almost as well, but he's never had Hugo's fluency."

She reached up to a cupboard, searched for something and then gave a sound of irritation.

"Mother, you didn't put coffee on the list, but I can't find any here."

"I don't wonder, dear. There isn't any. I'm so sorry. I finished the last of it this morning. I'm sure Mr. Netherford will like tea just as well."

Edward, asked, said untruthfully that of course tea would be fine.

Estelle took down a frying pan from a hook and took an egg from the refrigerator.

"Free range," she told Edward. She cut two slices of bread and put them into the toaster. "I get them from a farm a mile away."

"That's a very neat vegetable patch," he said. "I saw it through my window. Does your grandfather do it all himself?"

She nodded.

"All himself. He sells most of it, but he keeps us in vegetables all the year round. It's

42

a lot of work, but he enjoys it. Have you got a garden?"

"No. I live in rooms."

"Aren't you married?"

"No."

"I would have thought rooms were a bit dreary—but if they're service rooms, they do everything for you, don't they?"

"Everything," he said, and tried to keep the pleasure out of his voice.

She was putting bacon into the pan. She moved easily, and there was a deftness in the way she handled the things she was using. He began to realise that although there was a general air of untidiness in the room, everything that belonged to the children was in good order. Their mugs were washed, their plates clean; when the refrigerator was open, he could see their food neatly laid out. The children, he concluded, came first in this household.

She broke an egg neatly in half.

"Perhaps I should have given you two," she said.

"One will be enough, thank you."

"It wouldn't have been enough for my husband. He could be said to have eaten only one meal a day, and that was breakfast. No lunch, no tea, and a token dinner. He—oh!"

She broke off with an exclamation of annoyance.

"Toaster's giving trouble again," she told her mother. "I thought Grandad said he'd fixed it."

"It worked this morning," Mrs. Mallin reminded her.

"It won't work now."

"Never mind. The bread is so fresh, I'm sure Mr. Netherford would just as soon have it untoasted."

"Hobson's choice," said Estelle. "Will you carry your teapot into the living room?" she asked Edward. "Then sit down and I'll bring your egg and bacon."

He took the teapot, sat at the table laid for him, and waited. The bacon smelled good; the egg was sizzling. He began to feel better.

"Would you take Damien?" Mrs. Mallin asked Estelle. "I've got to get on with my work."

"Let me finish frying, then I'll take him," Estelle replied.

"He seems restless. You don't think he's coming in for a cold?"

"Let me look at him. No, I think he's all right. He's a bit overclothed, I think. It's going to be a hot day. We could—oh!"

She returned to the frying pan—somewhat

too late. The egg was hard and the bacon was burnt.

"I forgot to warm a plate," Estelle called to Edward. "Do you mind?"

"Not at all."

She came in carrying a cold plate with the egg and bacon on it. It did not look appetising.

"All we have for breakfast," she told him, "is cereal, which we eat while the children are having theirs. Then I drive into Balderwick— it's our nearest village—to do the shopping. We have a sandwich lunch."

He nodded, pouring out his tea and wistfully recalling avocado followed by a grilled sole, or a light soup followed by steak.

She had left him; she took the baby from her mother, and returned carrying it.

"I don't suppose you like babies," she said. "Bachelors usually don't. But for those who have eyes to see, and use them, this little fellow is a very fine specimen. He's going to be bigger than his brothers."

Edward was still hungry. He was about to ask for more bread when there came the sound of a prolonged blast on a motor horn.

"That's Tom!" she exclaimed. "Mother, Tom's come."

Tom was obviously a favourite with the entire household. Mr. Mundy had left his vegetable plot and was going with long strides to meet the car. The two small boys were running towards it uttering glad cries. Estelle opened a window of the living room and shouted.

"Hello, Tom. Come in."

But Tom, it appeared, was in too great a hurry to stop for long. He had driven by, he said, to see how they all were. He came up and spoke through the window. "Didn't get a chance to speak to you last night," he said. "So I thought—well . . ." his eyes opened wide at the sight of Edward. "Look who's here! Edward, how come?"

"He was sent here for bed and breakfast," Estelle said.

"God help him," said Tom piously. "Let me guess: burnt toast, soggy bacon and a ruined egg. Right?"

Edward had risen and was standing beside Estelle at the window.

"Wrong," she answered. "The toast wasn't burnt and the bacon was done to a turn."

"A miracle," Tom told Edward.

"How," Edward asked, "did you come out of last night's blaze?"

"Not too badly. Things are a lot better than I expected. I'm just going into town to talk about insurance. Want a lift?"

"Not in your car." Edward pointed to one of the back tyres, which was flat.

"That's fine." Tom sighed resignedly. "The spare tyre's got no air in it. I was going to have it filled in York. I'll have to travel with you, and I'll send out a man to fix my car."

"He may not be able to bring you back," Estelle said. "He's moving to a room in town."

"If he can get one," said Tom. "Which I doubt. If you get one, Edward, I'll take a taxi back."

"No need to do that. I'll run you back," Edward said.

He went to his room and came back carrying his case. He said goodbye to Estelle and Mrs. Mallin, paid what he owed, and thanked them for their hospitality. He made what he hoped were suitable noises of farewell to the children, and then with Tom beside him, drove in the direction of York.

As they went, Tom gave him a sidelong glance of amusement.

"Odd, your landing up at Pantiles," he said. "What did you make of them all?"

"Happy-go-lucky."

Tom considered this.

"Yes, I suppose you're right—up to a point," he concluded. "But there's more to them than that."

"You ought to know. They said you were their oldest—or was it best?—friend."

"Old Mr. Mundy has known me since I was born. I can remember Pantiles when it was a very small and ill-equipped bungalow."

"You couldn't call it ill-equipped now."

"No. All the improvements—and the additions to the house—were made by Estelle's husband."

"He wasn't around last night or this morning."

"And won't be. He's dead. He died a couple of months after Damien was born."

"Is Mrs. Mallin a widow too?"

"No. She divorced her husband. She didn't care much for marriage."

"Where's he now?"

"Isle of Skye. Living with a woman, but not married. He never leaves the island."

"What did Estelle's husband do for a living?"

"He started off as a master in a school in Exeter. Then he came to York and divided his time between writing mathematical text books and teaching. He was a visiting master at the school Estelle was at in York. That's how they met. She was seventeen and he was thirty-seven. A year later, they married. He inherited some money—not much—and the text books brought in something. He saw this half-derelict bungalow near Balderwick, bought it and spent most of his legacy doing it up and equipping it. Then they moved in."

There was a pause.

"Well, and then what?" Edward prompted. "He died?"

"No. He gave up teaching and settled down to the text books. He was a quiet sort of chap—ingrowing, introspective, whatever you like to name it—and he needed a peaceful background—hence the isolated bungalow. I think he imagined a life in which he'd write undisturbed and she'd run the house. But he reckoned without Nature."

"Babies?"

"That's right. I knew him well, and I'm certain that the thought of a family never entered his head. He waited apprehensively for the baby, and when it came—Hugo—discovered that his wife had a very strong maternal streak, and asked nothing more than to devote herself to her offspring. No sooner had Hugo started to crawl than she was pregnant again. When there was the certainty of a third baby, he lost his nerve."

"Three babies in four years. Did he leave her?"

"Not in so many words. He loved her, but

he knew he could never become a family man. He took a teaching job in Zimbabwe and said he'd send for Estelle and the babies when he found a house."

"But he didn't."

"He didn't get the chance. Whether he would have taken it or not, nobody'll ever know. He was killed in a taxi accident shortly after arriving in Harare. Estelle invited her mother and grandfather to come and share the bungalow with her."

"Where were they?"

"Living together in Whitby. There's not much money between the lot of them. Estelle just gets along. Her mother makes quite a good living making and selling picture frames to order. Grandfather sells vegetables. They're all extremely happy, Grandfather tending his cabbages, Mother in that kind of outhouse or cottage enjoying herself with frames, and Estelle looking after the babies and doing the family cooking and—now and then—tidying up the house. The outsider may not see much in the set-up to keep them happy, but there's an atmosphere about that establishment that you can only call . . . well, serene. Immured as they are—"

"Immured?"

"Well, they seldom go out. Estelle's life is

just the children."

"I suppose they tie her a great deal?"

"They don't tie her at all. She ties herself. I suppose she'll have a bit more time when they're old enough to go to school, but there's something about her that will keep the family united. When I said immured, I meant that they had very little social life. None of them wants it, or seems to need it. Old friends from Whitby drop in. Old school-friends turn up now and then. They're a musical trio— there's always a classical cassette playing in the background. They read newspapers and listen to the radio and keep up with the news, national and international. Not a bad life, but hardly one for a girl as young as Estelle."

"She's only—what? Twenty-three or twenty-four? She'll probably marry again, won't she?"

"If enough pressure's applied. She's had— she has—chances enough. I know three men who're wearing themselves out trying to convince her that the life she's leading isn't enough to absorb all her faculties. But we don't progress."

"We?"

"Of course, we. I've been after her since she grew up. Old Mundy would have liked to see us married, but she had a kind of father fixation, so she married the teacher of thirty-eight." He sighed. "Well, that's enough about that. What's brought you up north?"

"Business. I'm trying to wrest some heirlooms from a woman who's refusing to give them up. Her name's Brockman. Ever come across her?"

Tom shook his head.

"No. Where does she live?"

"In York. It's all rather a waste of time, but the three heirs came to see me and I have to do something about it."

"Young woman?"

"No. How long is it going to be before you can get that hotel going again?"

"I'll be able to answer that when I've talked to this builder fellow I know."

York was in sight. Edward slowed down.

"Where d'you want to be dropped?" he asked.

"Somewhere near the Minster."

Edward pulled out the notebook on which Mrs. Brockman's address was written.

"Know where this is?" he asked.

"Yes. Back of the Minster. A street near the Nursing Home. How about meeting me at a pub for a snack lunch?"

"Good idea."

"That one over there." Tom pointed to a small, picturesque, antique building nearby. "One o'clock?"

"Right. See you."

3

He found Mrs. Brockman's house without difficulty. It stood a little way back from the road—a quiet, narrow street without much traffic. There was a low wrought-iron gate. To this was affixed a large printed notice:

APOSTLES OF MELODY
All Welcome
11 a.m. to 1 p.m.

He hesitated, and then left his car behind a line of others. He glanced at the notice, opened the fastening of the gate, and walked up the path to the front door. He heard the buzz of many voices coming from inside. Through the windows of the two rooms in front of the house he could see people standing and looking uncomfortably cramped. This, he thought, was no time to approach Mrs. Brockman, but he had come all the way from London, and though she obviously could not give him her attention now, she might consent to make an appointment for the following day.

The front door was open, the hall filled with a crowd of men and women, all middle-aged or elderly, all wearing badges marked *A of M*.

Edward stopped on the threshold. Two women saw him, detached themselves from the crowd and joined him, their faces wreathed in smiles. They looked like mother and past-her-best daughter.

"*Another* one of us!" the older woman shrieked. It was not possible, in the din, to speak in normal tones. "You're late, you naughty man, you."

"And he's forgotten his badge," screeched the younger woman. "That was very, very risky. Mrs. Brockman told us particularly that everybody without a badge would be turned away. Shall we turn him away, Bessie?" she ended playfully.

"No. Let him come inside," said Bessie. "But where is his music? He's brought no music, June."

Edward noticed that every person in the hall was holding a roll of sheet music. The wild locks and strange attire of some of those present made him feel slightly nervous, and convinced him that he had made a mistake in intruding. He began to back out, but Bessie and June took his arms in a firm grip.

"Now don't be *silly*," said Bessie. "We didn't mean to hurt your feelings—did we, June?"

"No, we didn't," said June. "You can share my copy. In a few minutes we're going to get into line and sing the first number. We've never sung it before—not all together. You know the piece I mean—the one composed by Stanley Smythe—there he is, standing over there by the hatstand. It's the fourth piece he's composed for us."

"Third," corrected Bessie.

"*Fourth*, Bessie. You've forgotten—"

"Hush!" said Bessie. "We've got to line up. Come on."

There was a general move from the hall in the direction of the larger of the two front rooms. A tall, thin man with an almost totally bald head was in charge of the singers, shepherding them expertly into their places. Edward would have been drawn in if he had not firmly detached himself from Bessie and June.

He turned to leave—and then a voice halted him.

"Here, you!"

He looked round. The hall had emptied, but from the smaller room had come a short buxom woman with a face that would have looked pleasant and placid if it had not been marred by an expression of wrath.

"What are you doing here?" she demanded. "I've been watching you. No badge, no music. I know who you are—you're one of those nosey reporters."

"No." Edward faced her. "I assure you—"

"Don't bother to assure me." She spoke in a broad Yorkshire accent. "You can get out the way you got in. If you want to write anything in your notebook, you can say that this house was chosen for the first meeting of the Apostles of Melody. If you don't know what they are, I'll tell you: they're singers who gather into groups in their own towns to sing music that's been composed by one of their number. This is the first time they've come to York, and you can tell your paper that—"

"I'm not on any paper."

"You're not what?"

The singing had begun.

"I'm not," he said in his loudest tones, "on any paper. My name is Netherford."

A pause in the music made the last word a loud solo. Mrs. Brockman's eyes narrowed. She came close to him.

"You're that lawyer, aren't you?"

"I'm a lawyer, yes."

"And you sneaked in here, hiding yourself among the singers, to—"

"I'm sorry. I shouldn't have come in. But I thought that you might give me an appointment to see you some other—"

"Appointment? Out!" she commanded over a crescendo in the music. "Out! Leave at once."

The last words were again spoken into a pause in the music. The tall, thin man appeared in the hall, baton in hand.

"Could we have qui-ert?" he entreated. "You're interrupting the singing."

Mrs. Brockman lowered her voice to a menacing growl.

"Out! And double quick," she told Edward.

He turned, went out and walked to his car with as much dignity as he could muster. He drove along the road conscious that he had made a fool of himself—and he had probably ruined any chance he had of meeting her at an arranged interview. He could think of no way to erase the impression of this first visit.

He looked at his watch: midday. He felt angry and humiliated but above all, he felt hungry. A cup of tea, two slices of bread and some charred bacon and egg was no way to

58

begin a day. It was too early for Tom, but he would order something for himself.

But before eating, he should, he thought, do a round of the hotels and get himself a room. He drove to four—they were all fully booked, and the decisive manner in which he was turned away caused him to give up any further search. He would have to give way to the clergymen and the Apostles of Melody.

He went to the pub in which he and Tom had arranged to meet. He was glad to leave the heat of the street and find a comfortable chair in a room opening off the bar. He ordered beer and a double portion of sandwiches, and settled down to a meal which was a marked change from his well-chosen and well-served meals in London.

Tom came in when he was on his fifth sandwich. He stood by the chair, looked down at Edward and laughed.

"Bed but no breakfast," he said.

Edward nodded.

"Sorry I didn't wait for you."

"Not to worry." Tom took the adjacent chair. "I'll soon catch you up."

When he had given his order—two meat pies—he leaned back and stretched out his legs.

"I was laughing," he said, "because you're

the last person I would have committed to Estelle's ministrations. You're the type that likes his life well-ordered—as her husband did. You like the wheels of the domestic machine well-oiled. Well, you won't get that at Pantiles."

"You said she liked being a housewife."

"I said nothing of the sort. I said she liked her home. But she considers the home a place to be happy in. If there's any time over from looking after the babies, she'll do less important things like tidying up and putting things away and so on."

"To neglect the work of a house leads, in the end, to rather sordid conditions, doesn't it?"

Tom laughed again.

"That sounded like her husband talking," he said. "An old woman if ever there was one. If you don't watch out, you'll go the same way."

"What's wrong with keeping a house neat and tidy?"

"Nothing—if you like neatness and tidiness more than teaching babies how to walk, and watching their development. I'd rather have a good mother than a good housewife."

"I'd rather have both. Have you any idea how long these Apostles of Melody are going to grace this city?"

"No. All I know about them is that they're a pretty dedicated lot. They're quite untrained singers—middle aged and elderly—who've got members all over the place and who meet now and then to perform—not publicly—songs composed by themselves. They're fairly harmless, I gather."

"I walked into a meeting."

"Where?"

"At Mrs. Brockman's house. She turned me out. I was a fool to give her an excuse for not making an appointment to see me. Want another beer?"

"No, thanks. I'd rather get back. You don't have to take me."

"Yes, I do. I can't get into a hotel."

"So you're back at bed and no breakfast?"

"I'm afraid so."

They drove back together. It was just after two o'clock when they arrived. As they neared the house, Tom put out a hand and indicated that Edward was to slow down.

"Look at that," he said.

He was pointing to the field in which Pantiles stood. A rug was spread under a tree; on it was the remains of a picnic. Mrs. Mallin was on a deckchair some distance away, dozing in the sunshine. Her father was in another deckchair, a newspaper over his face, nodding.

The baby was asleep in its canvas cot. The two small boys lay on either side of Estelle, sending a ball to one another which she pretended to catch. It was a scene of open-air, sun-warmed leisure. Edward, letting his eyes range to the fields beyond, thought that his early opinion of this countryside had been mistaken. It was certainly flat—the Vale of York—but he now saw that it had a placid character of its own.

They got out of the car and joined the group on the rug. Tom could not stay long. The wheel of his car had been changed; he left with visible reluctance, and his last glance was for Estelle's graceful figure half lying, half seated on the rug.

"I'm afraid I couldn't get a hotel room," Edward said, when the car had driven away.

She spoke calmly.

"I didn't think you would. I'm sorry—for your sake. We're glad to have you back."

"That's very kind of you."

It sounded stiff, and far too formal for this easy, relaxed scene. But he had never found it easy to unbend, and this was the first time he had felt any real need to.

"Did you bring a cool shirt?" Estelle asked him. "If so, why don't you go and change into it?"

He went to the car, took out his suitcase, went to his room and emerged wearing a short-sleeved shirt and linen trousers.

"That's better," she said. "Sit down."

She patted the grass beside the rug, and he lowered himself and sat beside her. Hugo, after gazing at him for some time, gave him the ball.

"He thinks you're the athletic type," Estelle said. "Perhaps you are."

"Not really. Golf, tennis, squash—the usual."

"Did you get your interview with your client?"

"No. I walked in on an Apostles of Music session."

"Goodness!" Her eyes widened. "Did they sing?"

"They were beginning to when I left. I left by request."

"Thrown out?"

"Yes, more or less. I was a fool to barge in. With your permission, I'll phone and try to make an appointment for tomorrow."

She stopped the ball from going out of reach, held it and fixed her eyes on him in distress.

"Oh dear. I'm so sorry."

"What about?"

"There's no phone."

"No—"

"I mean, there's a phone, but it's been cut off. You see, I forgot to pay the bill, and they cut us off and it takes ages to get connected again." She sighed. "It's always happening."

"Always?"

"Well, every so often. I put the bills with all the other bills, and I mean to sit down and write cheques, but something always seems to come up. Like today. Would *you* do anything inside a house on a perfect day like this? No, you wouldn't. Or you shouldn't. Today is for breathing this gorgeous air and letting the sun soak into the children and me. Did you have a green salad with your lunch?"

"No."

"We had lettuce and watercress and endive and tomato, and new little green peas and bacon sandwiches, which are the boys' favourite meal. I think a lot of what's called children's diet is simply saving trouble by feeding them on cardboard cereals."

"I thought they were good for them."

"I didn't say they were bad for them. I'm just trying to say that if you use your imagination, you can make children's meals as interesting as your own."

Whatever she fed them on, he thought,

must be right. He had never seen a healthier trio.

"Didn't you manage to do what you came up to York to do?" she asked.

"No. I'll have to find the nearest phone and try to make an appointment for tomorrow."

"I'll take you. It's not far. The boys have to have a short sleep; when they wake up we'll have tea and then we'll put them in the pram and push them down to the post office."

"In Balderwick?"

"Yes. It's a small village, but it's got good shops. If I can't get what I want there, I drive into York. But for the shopping I do every morning, Balderwick's enough."

"Who are your nearest neighbours?"

"Farmers. We go past one of the farmhouses on the way to the shops. Sometimes we stop there. They've got Shetland ponies and the children are given rides on them. If you like riding, there are also horses there. Feel like a ride?"

"I don't think so, thank you."

She had risen and was clearing the rug of all the used plates and glasses and mugs. He helped her to carry them into the kitchen.

"Just put them anywhere you can find room," she said. "But not in the dishwasher— it's out of order."

She did not suggest washing up, but she selected from the assortment of crockery the things that had been used by the children. These she washed and dried and put away.

They went out to find that Mrs. Mallin had put the two boys on the rug to rest. Then she went back to her deckchair, and Estelle and Edward sat on the grass.

"We don't have to be quiet," she said. "If they're sleepy, they'll go off to the sound of drums. Whereabouts in London do you live?"

"Chiswick. With a view of the Thames."

"Do you have a daily woman to come and clean for you? No—you told me—you're in a service flat. Everything done."

"Practically everything."

"Washing and ironing?"

"No. The things go down the chute and are sent to the laundry."

"I'd like that—but not in a service flat. I'd want my own kitchen, and a large garden. And lots of light, airy rooms. In fact, I'd like this house with the service thrown in."

"You've lived here since you were married, haven't you?"

"We moved in—my husband and I—the day the builders moved out."

"Tom told me he did a lot to the place."

"He did everything—modern plumbing,

extra rooms with bathrooms, central heating, and every labour-saving machine on the market. He said the thing was to get the house right, and then working in it would present no difficulties."

She was leaning back on her hands, her face lifted to the sun. The children were asleep.

"It's certainly an easy-to-work house," she went on. "When I look back I wish—sometimes, not always—that I'd kept it as he thought I'd keep it. Immaculate."

"But something always came up?"

She laughed—a sound full of melody, he thought.

"Something always came up," she admitted. "But I saw to it that he could work quietly in his study, revising all his text books. It's such a shame he didn't want children. It's strange"—she turned and faced him—"he never looked beyond marriage. Marry the girl of his choice, make an ideal home for her, and proceed to live an orderly existence. But children aren't naturally orderly—don't you find that? Oh, I forgot. You haven't got any. I couldn't imagine life without them. It was a jolt for my husband when Hugo arrived, but he accepted him as he would have accepted any other hobby I went in for. Then Maurice appeared. Near panic. The thought of a third baby was the last straw. We talked it over, but he found that I wasn't the daughter-figure he'd taken me for. I was all set to go on producing more Hugos and more Maurices. So he begged to be excused."

She paused. She was gazing straight ahead. Edward realised that she had forgotten him in recalling the past.

"So the marriage, if you can call it that," she went on, "came to a dignified end. He packed all his personal belongings into trunks, settled a sum of money on me and the children, and turned his face to Zimbabwe and a tranquil future. I saw him off at the airport. He looked very happy. He was borne away in a jet, and by sea went all his neatly packed, neatly labelled trunks. That's how they came back to me after he was killed in a taxi accident in Harare. Still neat, still orderly—but a reminder that you can't take it with you."

There was silence. He found nothing to say. After a while, she shook herself out of a reverie and looked at him.

"What started me off on that?" she asked him. "I hardly ever think about it and I never talk about it—especially to strangers."

He realised, with a feeling of surprise, that he did not feel like a stranger. Something about this peaceful scene, this pastoral setting, appealed to part of him that he did not know existed. The hours he spent out of doors were spent on a golf course or a tennis court. Occasional picnics had been held in choice spots and furnished with appetising varieties of food and wine. He could not remember sitting on the grass with nothing to do but watch three children sleeping and their elders taking their ease. He had the feeling—unusual for him—that any work he had to do could wait until he was in the mood to do it. For the moment, there was the sun and a slight, cooling breeze and a girl beside him who was utterly unselfconscious, utterly direct, a girl unlike any he had met before.

"I suppose," he asked her, "you went straight from school into marriage?"

"Not quite," she answered. "My mother got alarmed because I'd seen so little of the world—she meant the world beyond classrooms. She and my grandfather got together and emptied their piggy banks and sent me to Italy. They hoped I'd get this older man out of my mind and find a younger one. But I didn't change my mind. When I married, I didn't have far to move. My husband had bought this house and done it up, and I only had to come from Whitby. I was brought up in my grandfather's house there. Very small, but on a road with the sea splashing below. When my husband died, I asked my mother and grandfather to come and live here with me, so they came. It's worked very well—Grandad's making money selling his vegetables and my mother—she does picture framing—has clients all over Yorkshire. In between framing, she makes all our clothes. She loves clothes. She's what you might call an elegant dresser—even when she's cutting glass and carving frames. End of biography, and time to make some tea."

The breeze had freshened. The newspaper blew off Mr. Mundy and was gently replaced by his daughter. The baby stirred and woke. Estelle lifted him from his cot.

"I'm going to take him inside and change him," she said. "If you put on the kettle and find some cups, we'll bring the tea out here."

After changing the baby's nappy, she found that the two boys had wakened. She brought them in and washed their faces, and while she did so, Edward was left to make the tea. He searched for and found cups and mugs and teapot and milk jug, put them on to a tray and carried it out and deposited it on the rug. Mrs. Mallin came over to pour out the tea.

"If I'd known you were doing this all by

yourself," she said, "I would have gone in and helped you."

He doubted it. She had looked very settled in her deckchair.

Mr. Mundy woke up, and his tea was carried to him. The rest sat round the rug, the baby in its cot between his mother and Edward. Then Estelle and Edward and the children started out for the walk to Balderwick to telephone.

The post office was a combined newsagent's, stationer's and confectioner's, with a small cage at the end of the shop in which was a middle-aged woman with a cheerful countenance. There was considerable delay before Edward's business was attended to—the babies were the centre of attention, and it became clear to Edward that all three were well acquainted with both postmistress and customers. At last his call was put through and he was sent to a telephone situated in a distant corner. He heard Mrs. Brockman's voice.

"Who is it?"

"My name is Netherford. I'm sorry I disturbed you this morning, but—"

"I suppose you've got to see me?"

"If you could make an appointment—"

"Who sent you? Those three who're after the pictures?"

"They—"

71

"I'll be here tomorrow at five. You can come if you want to, but I'm warning you it won't do any good. I've made my plans and you're not going to talk me out of them. And that's all I'll say to you now. Except one thing: you're wasting my time and you're wasting your own."

She rang off. Edward joined the party waiting on the pavement.

"Everything all right?" Estelle asked.

"More or less. I've made an appointment for tomorrow evening."

"Does that mean we'll have you for tonight? Good. I've bought a new toaster. The old one had been to the mender's too many times. It needed pensioning off. Now let's go home."

4

The walk back to the house, skirting the river, along roads almost devoid of traffic, was a slower procession than the walk to the post office had been. The two boys, tired of the pram, were allowed to walk. The baby sat upright and amused himself by throwing his teddy bear on to the road and watching Edward pick it up and restore it to him, to be immediately hurled out again.

"Can't you stop him from doing that?" Edward asked Estelle at last.

"You try," she invited.

"You could tie the bear on to a short string," he suggested.

"Don't be a kill-joy. That takes away all the fun. I thought you were enjoying the bending exercise."

The next time he had to retrieve the bear, he hid it behind his back and indicated that

it had gone for ever. There was a peaceful interlude during which the baby bent over the sides
of the pram and tried to see where it had gone.

"On walks like this," Estelle said, "I miss
dogs. My husband outlawed animals."

"Why?"

"Hygiene. He said that babies and dogs
didn't go well together."

"Why not?"

"I'm talking about dogs that are allowed
into the house. Real doggy dogs. But I had to
agree that they had their drawbacks. They
licked the baby's face. They left hairs on the
carpets that the baby crawled on. They got
playful and knocked the baby down when he
was learning to stand up. They brought mud
into the hall. They made off with the baby's
toys and hid them, the way you're hiding that
bear. So I agreed no dogs. But I still miss
them. When the children are older, I'm going
to readmit them. Puppies and kittens. I suppose you can't keep dogs, living in service
rooms."

"No."

"Don't you ever want to live in a house with
a big garden?"

"No. I'm very comfortable as I am."

"It sounds a nice life. Office—and golf and
tennis and squash. How about night life?"

"Parties now and then."

"Do you take one girl out, or do you, as they say, play the field?"

"I have women friends, if that's what you mean."

"It isn't quite what I mean. But my grandfather's always telling me that there are people—like you—who answer questions but don't volunteer personal information, and who don't spill all their life history, as I do, on first meeting. But if you don't volunteer, how can anyone make up their minds as to what you're like?"

"There are such things as—"

"I know. Ships that pass in the night. But you didn't. You stayed, and I find you interesting because you're such an old friend of Tom's. Didn't you ever lose touch with him?"

"No. We didn't often meet, but there was a time when we were always together."

"At school?"

"No. Afterwards. We went on trips together—France, Spain, Italy, Turkey."

"I knew he'd been away with a friend, but I didn't know who the friend was."

The two boys were lagging behind. She picked up one, Edward picked up the other and they were deposited in the pram and the teddy bear restored on condition that it was not thrown out. The three were, he thought, unusually good-tempered children. Apart from the baby's outburst when he was teething, there had been little quarrelling and no complaining. Like their mother, they had an air of finding the world a pleasant place.

The house came into view, and the boys began to utter cries of delight. On the field was a man holding a beautiful Shetland pony. Beside him was Mrs. Mallin.

"Brian," said Hugo.

"Yes, it's Brian," agreed his mother.

"And horse."

"Pony," she corrected.

She lifted him and his brother out of the pram, and they ran to the gate and scrambled between the bars, shouting a welcome.

The man was about Edward's age, suntanned, fair, cleanshaven and wearing jodhpurs and a shirt. Tethered nearby was his own mount—a chestnut. He lifted each child in turn and held him over his head. He patted the baby's head, glanced past Edward and fixed his eyes on Estelle. The expression in them left Edward in no doubt that here was a rival to Tom.

"Hi, Estelle," he greeted her.

His demeanour was confident—a shade too confident, Edward thought. He had none of

Tom's quiet, easygoing manner. When Estelle introduced Edward, he gave him no more than a nod in acknowledgment.

"I brought the pony over to give the children rides," he told Estelle. "You said that this was the best time."

"It is. You be the groom and I'll get the children's supper ready."

Brian frowned.

"Not yet," he said. "You've got to stay and see how they get on."

"That's right, Estelle." It was Mrs. Mallin speaking. "I'll get the children's supper ready. And perhaps Mr. Netherford would come and help me."

For a moment Edward could not believe his ears. A hint was a hint, but he had never been given a broader one. He felt trapped.

"I'm afraid I'm no good at—" he began.

But Mrs. Mallin had slipped her hand under his arm and was propelling him towards the house.

"Poor Brian," she explained on the way, "gets so little time with Estelle. He's so kind—he's always suggesting coming over with a pony and giving the children rides—and sometimes he even persuades her to go out to dinner with him. Not often; she doesn't like leaving the children, not even with me and her grandfather."

77

She was putting the children's mugs on the small table. Edward was standing gazing at the unwashed crockery to be seen everywhere. Perhaps she read his thoughts.

"We usually do all the washing up at night, when we've finished dinner," she told him. "At the moment, the dishwasher is out of order. Sometimes we stack the used things, and sometimes we don't. I suppose you don't have to do any housework?"

"No."

"If you moved to a house when you married, you'd have to, I suppose."

He was looking out of the window. Hugo was being held on the pony by his mother. Brian was leading the pony and Maurice was dancing along beside them.

"What's his other name?" he enquired.

"Brian's? Van Leyden—his ancestors were Dutch. He owns that farm about a mile away from here—a beautiful place. Perhaps Estelle pointed it out to you as you went by. Brian inherited it when he was twenty. He's a good farmer—and, I might add, very rich."

Two very eligible suitors, Edward mused. Tom—and van Leyden. She could marry either of them and employ housekeepers to do the washing up and look after the children—though he doubted, even from the little he knew of her, whether she would hand over the babies to anybody.

She did not come in until Brian had ridden away with the pony on a leading rein. Edward had tired of gazing at the dirty plates and was stacking them in neat piles on the side of the sink. She watched him in surprise.

"If I thought that all bed and breakfasters did that," she commented approvingly, "I'd go into business."

"Did Brian suggest dining out?" Mrs. Mallin asked her.

"He did."

"What did you say?"

"I told him I was cooking dinner for my paying guest."

"Speaking of payment," Edward said, "You've not given me a definite figure yet."

"I didn't have one to give you. I had to ask at the post office what the going rate was. I'll charge that and subtract something for lack of home comforts. Do you want to go into York for dinner, or are you having it here?"

"Here, if it's no trouble."

"Can you eat a cheese soufflé? It might not rise, but it'll still be cheesy. And soup—nice fresh vegetable soup. And while I get it ready, you can go out and talk to my grandfather."

Edward found Mr. Mundy placing a folding

table on the edge of the field, and carrying out bottles and glasses.

"This," he told Edward, "is the only time of day we foregather for a drink. The baby goes to sleep, the boys go to bed, and my daughter and granddaughter and I sit down to sherry. Indoors, unless we get a warm evening like this one."

Edward brought over the deckchairs and Mr. Mundy carried an easy chair out from the house. Then he and Edward sat down with their drinks beside them.

"Nice part of the world, this," the old man said contentedly. "Cold in winter, but open and healthy. It's pretty flat round here, but as you probably know, there's beautiful country within easy reach."

"I know. Yorkshire's always been my favourite county. But my father preferred Somerset."

"You were at school in Yorkshire?"

"Yes. With Tom."

Mr. Mundy sipped his sherry.

"He's a nice fellow, Tom," he said. "He was an attractive child and a nice boy and he grew into—well, you know him as well as I do. I don't mind telling you, on the quiet, that I once thought he'd be the right husband for Estelle—but she chose an older man. Pity.

It was a dull life, in some ways—but she didn't find it dull. None of us—Celia, Estelle, myself—care much for what you might term diversion. Do you think she's too young to settle down to a life like the one she's living?"

"Yes."

Mr. Mundy smiled.

"So does everybody else. But how does one persuade her to remarry? She's got all she wants."

"The children? She can't keep them when they're older."

"You mean she shouldn't."

"I suppose that's what I mean. I'd say—now that you've asked me—that this is rather a narrow life for her."

Mr. Mundy was silent for a while.

"It's odd, isn't it?" he said at last. "People have grown away from the Victorian ideals."

"And a good thing too."

"Yes. A good thing. But the kind of home people live in nowadays—I'm talking about people in the middle-income range—doesn't, I think, offer the security that children felt in those Victorian settings. Parents have changed."

"Not parents. Mothers."

"All right. Mothers. If they don't want a career, they want a husband who takes a half share in the housework. They want to enter-tain—I suppose you're always being invited to those foreign-food dinners. They want holidays abroad. They perhaps want children, but the children are made to fit into the life style."

"It's a wider life than it used to be."

"Yes," Mr. Mundy conceded. "And no. I can't help feeling that people ask too much. They don't keep up with the Joneses any more—they outstrip them. What people call happiness, today, isn't happiness. It's enjoyment. It's pleasure. And between happiness and pleasure there's a very large gap. There's"— he broke off apologetically. "Good Lord, I'm getting prosy. Here—let me refill your glass."

"You all," Edward said, holding it out, "seem very happy."

"We are. What you're seeing is three examples of job-satisfaction. What we do, we like doing."

"And what you do, you seem to me to do well."

Mr. Mundy chuckled.

"There's a catch in that 'what you do'," he said. "We should do a great deal more. But the house gets a face-lift when Estelle notices how much dust has gathered. And when this field gets too overgrown, I call in a chap who knows how to wield a scythe. I would have liked to get a flower garden going, but I found I couldn't do both—flowers and vegetables. So I opted for the vegetables."

"And a nice neat plot you've got," Edward said.

Their talk, easy, desultory, was interrupted by the arrival of Mrs. Mallin.

"I've been sent away," she said. "Estelle says it doesn't take two to make a soufflé."

"Children in bed?" her father enquired.

"And asleep. That pony ride did them good."

Estelle joined them some time later. Like her mother, she had changed into a summer dress. She stayed briefly for a drink. Edward, remembering the soufflé, appointed himself timekeeper, and soon they all went indoors to a meal which Edward found to be of a standard considerable higher than that of breakfast.

The evening grew chilly. Mrs. Mallin and her father put on coats and returned to their deckchairs. Edward and Estelle strolled up the road in the opposite direction to that which they had taken earlier.

"Why," she asked, "have you come all this way to see a client? I thought clients called on their lawyers."

"I'm taking over at the second stage—trying

to induce someone to part with three pictures."

"Valuable?"

"Reasonably. Genuine Impressionists, but not well known."

"We never had any good pictures. We never had any good anything—except books. There were always plenty of those. My grandfather, my mother, myself—and my husband. Only his were mostly on mathematics."

"Do you miss him?" he found himself asking.

Her answer was unhesitating.

"No. It wasn't the sort of marriage you'd miss. And his wasn't a presence you'd miss. He was quiet and retiring and always absorbed in his work. He didn't want to be interrupted, or asked about anything to do with the house." She sent a glance at him. "I imagine you're rather like that. Are you?"

"Quiet and retiring?"

"No. Not wanting to be bothered by household matters. But you don't know, do you? Your life isn't tied up with domesticity."

"I suppose not." He paused. "If you ever go to London, I hope you'll let me know. I should like to see you again," he ended.

The words hung in the air. He wondered whether he had uttered them. He deplored her untidiness, her lack of method. He considered her devotion to her children excessive, unwise and short-sighted. He thought her good looking, but he was disconcerted by the way she presented herself to the world just as she was, without adornment or assumed social graces. One part of him regretted having to leave this unusual household, but on the whole, he thought, it would be a relief to get back to people who conformed to what he looked on as normal behaviour. He had an appointment with Mrs. Brockman tomorrow, and after it he would go straight back to London. He could, with luck, be in time to order dinner in his rooms.

"What did you think of Brian van Leyden?" he heard her asking.

"I didn't see him for more than a few minutes. Then your mother removed me in order to leave you alone with him."

"He's her favourite."

"Favourite candidate for your hand? Myself, I prefer Tom."

"So does my grandfather. But Brian's—"

"—got a lot going for him? Well, he's rich and he's a good farmer and he's kind to your children. Anything else?"

"He didn't have a very good time when he was at school. His parents were separated, and always left him at school for holidays. He—"

She stopped. A car had driven up beside them. Tom, at the wheel, switched off the engine and leaned out to address them.

"Just missed you at the house," he told Estelle. "I wanted a word with Edward."

"Well?" Edward asked.

"Would you take on the job of sorting out some tricky claims I've got tied up in? Not insurance claims—those'll be straightforward enough. These are more personal—members of the staff who've suffered losses too trivial to turn over to the insurance fellows, but which I'd like to do something about."

"Not a lawyer's job, is it?" Edward asked.

"Not strictly—but some points of law are creeping in, and I'd like your advice. I'll even pay for it."

"I'll see you do. Can you run down to London to see me?"

"No. I'm what the Americans call hog-tied. I was hoping you'd come to me. For a fat fee, of course."

"I'd have to—"

"I know. Go back first. But couldn't you come up again, fairly soon? You could make it a weekend if it suited you better."

Edward took a few moments to consider.

He felt a curious elation at the thought of returning.

"I'd have a room at the hotel ready for you," Tom said. "Think it over."

"I don't need to think it over. But I can't give you a definite return date at the moment."

"I understand that. Thanks for not turning it down." He switched on the engine. "Want a lift back to the house?"

Edward said that he would like to go on walking. He helped Estelle into the car and stood in the road watching it drive away, conscious that for the second time in one evening, he was stepping aside in order to let a suitor have his say.

He was up early next morning, to a day that looked as bright and felt as warm as the previous one had been. It was hard to believe that he had arrived so recently under monsoon conditions.

He heard no sound in the house. When he was dressed, he walked to the kitchen and saw that Estelle had washed and dried the children's breakfast mugs and plates and was putting on their jerseys in preparation for going out. She looked at Edward in surprise and some dismay.

"Good morning. I didn't think you'd be up

so early. Do you want your breakfast?"

"Not until the shopping's done. I thought it might be a change for you all to go in my car."

"The boys would love it."

"I saw your grandfather had made a start on the vegetable garden."

"He's always early. My mother drove into York to deliver some orders."

Arriving in Balderwick, Edward found that the children knew every stallholder or shop-keeper that Estelle dealt with. Edward kept his eye on them, and carried the purchases to the car. They were home within the hour. The baby was put in the pram, the boys ran free with Mr. Mundy keeping watch over them. Estelle put coffee and fresh bread on to the table. He leaned over to get the bread board and knife.

"With your permission," he said, "I'm going to make my own breakfast."

"Go ahead." She pointed to the new toaster. "Look. If you hadn't been here, we would have taken the old one to be fixed yet again, and while we were waiting for it to come back in the same condition it was in when it sent, we'd have done without toast."

He was making coffee, and she watched him admiringly.

"You're handier that I thought you were," she said. "When did you last make your own breakfast?"

"Camping at the beginning of May."

"Where?"

"Down in Cornwall. There were four of us."

"Two couples?"

"Yes. A music professor and his wife, and their niece—and me. Could I have another egg? I'm rather hungry."

She gave him one, and he cooked both with bacon and a tomato.

"Sure you won't join me?" he asked.

"Quite sure. I don't like breakfast. I had coffee before you were up. But I'll have some more if there's enough."

He poured out a cup for her and then looked about him as if in search of something.

"What are you looking for?"

"A tray. This is too good a morning to miss. If you'll load the tray, I'll carry out that folding table."

They sat in the sunshine, and the children came to watch them. Life, Edward thought, was very pleasant on a day like this. Flourishing vegetables, healthy babies, fresh bread and a girl who looked her best in sunlight.

"You're tanned," he told her.

"I always go brown and not red, I'm glad to

say. Your colouring's rather like mine. We've both got blue eyes and fair hair. Have you got any sisters or brothers?"

"No."

"Mother and father?"

"No."

"Aunts and uncles?"

"Distant. I had a godfather, but he died. He left me his money, which was nice of him. I used some of it to buy myself into the firm. Do you think you'll ever get as far as London? I'd like to show you round."

"That's what Tom's always saying—show me round."

"Show you the sights."

"York's the place for that. I wonder how many times I've been round the Minster and St. William's College? I love York. In fact, I love Yorkshire."

"If you—" he began, and stopped. A car was at the gate and a man was getting out. He approached the table, bowed ceremoniously to Edward and then took Estelle's hand and dropped some kisses on the palm.

"Who," he asked, indicating Edward, "is this fellow?"

"His name is Edward Netherford and he's a lawyer who came from London two days ago. This," she told Edward, "is Anthony

Brewster, who owns an antique shop in York, full of lovely things."

Selling antiques, Edward thought as he studied the sleek, long-nosed car, must be a profitable business.

"I came," Anthony said, "because you thought you might be able to come out to lunch with me today."

"Oh, Anthony—I forgot!"

"She forgot." Anthony was addressing Edward. "She forgot. A man asks her out, she gives him enough hope to keep him keyed up for a week—and then she says, with no sign of remorse, that she forgot."

"It couldn't have been today, Anthony. This is the day my mother had to go to York, and I knew she'd be having lunch out."

"It *was* today," Anthony told her firmly. "And you forgot. I suppose you forgot to pay the telephone bill again, thus making it impossible for anybody to get through to you."

He was shorter than Edward, with grey eyes and fair hair and a misleading look of innocence.

"You up here on business?" he asked Edward.

"Yes."

"He's got an appointment with a client at five o'clock today," Estelle said. "He went to

91

see her, and ran into a meeting of the Apostles of Melody."

"And a ruddy great nuisance they are," Anthony said. "Singers! They swarm into a town and grab most of the available accommodation. They're all over the place—they, and the clergymen. I ought to like singers—I was called Rooster at school, which gives you some idea of what my voice is like. Incidentally, there's a circus out near the river. No use offering to take Estelle's children—she's anti circus, and teaching her children to be."

"Anti circus and anti all performing animals, and anti bullfights," Estelle said.

"Go on—you haven't listed them all yet," Anthony said. "Anti animals in small apartments, anti birds in cages, and a whole lot more. Estelle, my darling, I've got to get back to the shop. Are you sure lunch is off?"

"Yes. I'm sorry, Anthony."

"You're not standing me up in order to go out with this lawyer chap?"

"No."

"Then I'll say goodbye. I hope," he told Edward, "you won't come back. I'm still trying to work out why you're having breakfast here."

"I'm a bed and breakfaster," Edward told him.

"You're what?"

"He's my first, and I think my last bed and breakfast guest," Estelle said. "I put my name on the list ages ago, and he rode in on the storm the other night."

"Little knowing what he was in for. Let it be a lesson to you," he warned Edward. "She's a lovely girl, a kind and warm-hearted girl, but the only real interest in her life is those three infants you see over there. Now I'm off. I'll drop in during the week, Estelle darling."

This time, he kissed her cheek. Then he crossed the field to the gate, stopped to salute Mr. Mundy and do some shadow-boxing with the two boys, and got into his car.

"He's more sensible than he sounds," Estelle said, waving as the car went out of sight. "You should go to his shop—it's full of beautiful things. He doesn't like selling them—he likes travelling all over the world collecting them. Some of them are in his house, but not many. He lives in a minor mansion on the other side of York—big rooms with very little in them—the occasional statue here and there, men in armour, tapestries on the walls. Picturesque, but not homey. Not a house I could live in."

That, Edward concluded, made its owner's chances look dim.

"Are you going straight back to London

after seeing your client?" she asked.

He spoke with decision.

"Yes. I think I'd better get back."

"That means goodbye for ever," she said. "It's not likely that the Apostles of Melody will ever clash with an influx of clergymen again. And Tom's hotel won't burn down again—we hope—so there'll be lots of places for you to stay in."

"I suppose so. I'm very grateful for what you've done."

"That's polite, but I didn't do much. Come and see us when you come up to do this work for Tom."

"Thank you. I'd like to."

That was not all he wanted to say—but it was all he managed to say.

5

When he reached it that evening, the house near the Minster looked to him larger than it had done when he had seen it filled with the Apostles of Melody. As he walked to the front door, it was opened by Mrs. Brockman, and he had to complete the journey with her eyes fixed on him.

"Come in," she said.

He entered the hall and she closed the door behind him.

"This way," she said, and led him to the larger of the two front rooms, which he now saw to be a drawing room with heavy furniture and chairs that proved more comfortable than they looked.

"Sit down," she said.

He took a chair and she sat on a sofa opposite.

"First," she said, "I'm going to make you an apology."

"I don't see—"

"I was rude to you. You took me by surprise."

Her face, no longer red and angry, he saw to be round, clear-skinned and brown-eyed. Her nose was too small, her mouth too large, but he was slowly getting the impression of a pleasant and friendly woman.

"I knew they'd send a lawyer. They said they were going to," she went on. "But I didn't expect him to appear all mixed up with those singers. I only had them here because my sister asked me to. She's a widow, like me. She lives near Durham. She said all they wanted was a few people in the towns they visited who'd let them have a room to sing in, and give them some sandwiches and lemonade when it was all over. When they turned up, I was sorry I'd agreed to have them. A lot of cranks, they looked. But they were a harmless lot. If they want to get together and sing, I'm not going to stop them. Only trouble was that they came here when there were all these clergymen around. These streets are too narrow to take crowds. Have you had your tea?"

"Yes, thank you."

"I have mine at six—high tea, you'd call it. That's why I fixed five o'clock for you to come. Between your tea time and mine. And

96

now—" she settled herself with her feet planted firmly on the carpet—"we can come down to business. You must be the son of the Mr. Netherford who used to look after Mr. Brockman's legal work."

"Yes."

"What happened to him?"

"He died."

"I'm sorry about that. He was a nice helpful gentleman. It was him who used to keep the peace between those three younger Brockmans and me. D'you know them well?"

"Hardly at all. They came to me—"

"That's right. It was in the last letter I had from them. 'Put it into the hands of our lawyer' was what they said. So you're here to collect those three pictures, and you expect me to make a parcel of them and let you carry them out under your arm."

"I hoped that—"

"I'm not giving them up. Not yet awhile." She sounded quiet but determined. "They're all I've got to give me a chance to get some of my own back on those three sneering snobs. How much do you know of this business?"

"All there is to know, I think. You were employed as housekeeper at the Brockman house in London. During this time, Mr.

Brockman's wife died. Some time later, he married you."

"That's right. And left his house and came up to live in this one. I lived here with my first husband, and he died and left it to me; house, contents—the lot. I suppose you know I was married before I married Mr. Brockman?"

"Yes."

"It was him dying—my first, I mean—that made me think of working again. I'd worked all my life—well, since I was sixteen—and when I was left a widow, I found I didn't have enough to do to keep me busy. I wasn't old—I was twenty years younger than Mr. Brockman. Just fifty, I was, when he married me. So I began looking round for a job, and then I saw this advertisement for a housekeeper. I'd been cook-housekeeper in my other jobs, but I thought it would be a nice change to drop the cooking part. So I went to London and had an interview. With Mr. Brockman. The other three didn't show themselves. If they had, things would've turned out differently, because from the first look, I took against them. You've seen them—a mean-looking lot, and you can't deny it."

Edward did not attempt to. He was feeling more and more that in this fight, if fight it could be called, he was on her side. There was something about her that he could not yet name—he labelled it something between integrity and wholesomeness.

She was going on without pause.

"It sounded a good job. I could see from the house and the things in it that they had money. They paid top wages to three servants: cook, parlourmaid, housemaid—but they couldn't keep them. They all came—and went. So they thought a housekeeper might do the trick, stop the rot, get the staff to stay. If I'd been using my head, I would've wondered why four able-bodied people needed three resident servants in these days, when most people have to get along with a daily. But I was thinking what a nice man Mr. Brockman was—I liked him from the first—and so I took the job. My sister was a widow—I told you—and I asked her to come and live in this house and keep an eye on it until my working days, as you might say, were over. So she came, and I went."

"You were there for—"

"Three years. Three hard, long years. If I hadn't had the disposition I've got—happy, or at any rate cheerful—I'd have given up after the first month. No, that's not true—I was getting to like old Mr. Brockman more and more. It got so I couldn't bring myself to give in my notice. Then his wife died, and things came out right into the open and he said he wouldn't be able to stand the house without me, and would I marry him, and I said straight out: 'Yes. I'm fond of you,' I told him, 'but stay in this house I won't. I've got a nice house in York, and we can both live there and be happy.'"

"So he made a new Will."

"Right. Everything went to those three—I didn't want any of it. All the money went to them too, all except enough to arrange an annuity for me so I need never worry about that side of things again. The only possessions he brought up north were the three pictures he'd had left to him by the first Mrs. Brockman. He treasured those paintings. Used to sit for hours on end just looking at them."

"Left to him for his lifetime, but—"

"—but to go to his children—one each—when he died. So we got married and came here, and the pictures came with us. They hung in the dining room and there they are to this day. And now you've come to get them."

"I came—"

"You came for nothing, because I'm not going to give them to you. Or to anyone else, legal or not—until *I* decide to."

"But—"

"Wait a minute. I haven't finished. I've told you the whole story because I want you to know a bit about what I went through when I was with the family in London. I'm not over-sensitive, and I've got a fairly good picture of myself, and I know what I am and what I'm not. But I've had respect paid to me all my life—and respect is what I thought was my due. Just common politeness, that's all I've ever asked. But what did I get from those three? Not a welcome, not a pleasant word—just snubs. They treated me like they'd treated all the servants who'd upped and left. Dirt under their feet, and that's no exaggeration. I stood it because of their father—and not being blind, they must have seen he was coming to be fond of me. They would have got rid of me—but maybe you don't know what they're like. Selfish, and fond of their comforts. The idea of going back to servants who left as soon as they appeared was too much for them. I was making up to their father—so they thought—and they thought that by speaking against me they could get him to think as they did. It didn't work. But they made my life as difficult as they could, and it's because I put up with so much from them that I'm going to see to it that they put up with something from me for a change. Do you blame me, Mr. Netherfall?"

"Ford. I sympathise with you—"

"I don't want sympathy. I want understanding."

"I understand that you bear them a grudge. You—"

"It isn't a grudge. It's something else. I want to get my own back, not only on my account, but for Mr. Brockman as well. They put him through it, same as me. So I'm not going to hand over those pictures until I've given them a fright. You can tell them I've burned them, if you like. Not that I would. Mr. Brockman thought a lot of them."

"Did he ever have them valued, do you know?"

"No. Not in my time. I don't know much, but I know enough they're painted by what's called Impressionists. Only not well known ones, Mr. Brockman said."

"You understand, of course, that—"

"I know what you're going to say. The law. I've been round asking questions. First there's you. You don't get the pictures and I tell you I'm keeping them, so you go away and write me some more letters, and then there's things like court orders and writs.

But those—writs—have to be handed over personally, and I'm not going to be available when someone comes along with one. If you want to know, I'm going to do a disappearing act. I plan to ask my sister to come and stay in this house and I'm going away—and I'm going to take those three pictures with me. I'm sorry if this is going to give you any trouble. I like you. I always know at once if I like someone or if I don't. It was because I liked the look of you that I let you come here this evening."

"Thank you. But—"

"There's nothing more to say, Mr. Nettleford. My mind's made up."

"Nether."

"That's what I said—Nettleford. I'm sorry for you, having to deal with those three. But I suppose you can't turn the job down. You have to take what comes, like doctors and dentists."

"Those three, as you call them, have the law on their side."

"And a fat lot of good that'll do them. If things look like getting too near a court case, I'll part with the pictures. Not until. And that's the last word we need to say about it. I'm sorry you had your journey for nowt."

He rose. There seemed no point in prolonging the conversation. But she had an invitation to tender.

"Look here, Mr. Nettleford, why don't you stay and have tea with me? We set a good table up in these parts, and if you like good food, you'll like mine."

"I was—"

"Were you going straight back to London?"

"Yes."

"Then have something before you go."

She led him into the dining room, and the array of dishes on the table made his hesitation vanish. He could see fresh, homemade pork pies, thick slices of brown bread spread with butter, four different brands of cheese, an apple pie and a large brown teapot. Standing by her chair, she pointed to the wall behind Edward.

"There you are," she said. "Take a look."

He turned. The pictures were hung one above the other. The topmost depicted a girl walking through a field. The middle one was a group seated round a picnic on the sands. The third, the lowest was, in Edward's eyes, the most beautiful of the three—two young children looking over a wall. They wore large straw hats and pinafores, and as he gazed at them, he felt his first stirring of sympathy for the three owners, bereft of such a feast for the eyes.

Mrs. Brockman was watching him.

"This is the first time you've seen them?" she enquired.

"Yes. My father told me they were good, but I didn't expect . . . They're beautiful!"

"They are that," Mrs. Brockman agreed simply. "So I knew what I was doing when I decided to keep them for a while. It's going to hurt those three." She pointed to the food on the table. "Sit down. I'll make the tea," she invited. "I got this ready in case you'd stay and have a bite. I like company at meals. Have a good tuck-in."

He was surprised at how much he ate. In between mouthfuls, he answered her questions.

"You're a bachelor?"

"Yes."

"I guessed that. I can always tell. There's something about them. Do you share lodgings with someone?"

"No. I live in rooms."

"With service, of course."

"Yes."

"Whereabouts?"

"Cicero Mansions. They're—"

"I know where they are," Mrs. Brockman

interrupted. "Chiswick. My niece's husband is in charge of all the flats in it."

"Keaton?"

"That's him. Black. She met him up at Ilkley, and after waiting for her parents to get used to the idea, they got married and he got the Cicero Mansions job. I pop in and see them whenever I come to London—which isn't often. I'm not in favour of service flats. Go on too long being waited on, and you end up spoilt. D'you eat in or out?"

"I usually lunch at a small restaurant in Cleeve Street, near my office."

"When you get back, I suppose you've got to report to those three?"

"I shall write to them."

"They won't be pleased to know they've come to a stop. I hope they won't take it out on you."

He wiped his mouth on the large, hand-embroidered napkin.

"It seems," he said, "a lot of trouble for you to go to just to delay giving back the pictures."

"It's no trouble. It's a pleasure. You might say, in a way, that I'm being pig-headed. Well, that may be. All I know is that it's the only way I can get some of my own back for the way they treated me."

"I know that, but—"

"What I could never make out was why they thought they were such bigwigs. Their father was the son of a wholesale tea merchant. He was brought up in what you might call comfort, but not luxury. But the money kept coming in, and he married money—she was a baron's daughter, with a title, but I wouldn't have said that was enough to let them set themselves up like lords. They never—those three—said one polite word to me. They gave me orders with their noses stuck in the air—until they saw how things were going between their father and me. Then they would have sacked me, but he had some say in that."

"Why did you stay to be insulted?"

"For their father's sake, that's why. I'm speaking the truth when I tell you he needed me. And then we got out of that house and got married and I had some happy years with him, and now I'm going to hang on to those pictures for as long as I can."

He rose reluctantly from the table—there were still two pork pies left.

"Thank you for a splendid Yorkshire tea," he said.

"Come again some time when all this picture fuss is over. Where did you stay while you were here?"

"I had great difficulty in getting in any-where. Finally, I stayed for bed and breakfast at a house called Pantiles, out at—"

"Balderwick. I know it. A Mrs. Mallin and her daughter. I've never come across them but I've heard of them and I've seen them. The mother makes picture frames. Did they make you comfortable?"

"Very comfortable indeed," he lied. "But they don't take guests any more."

"There's an old man too, isn't there?"

"Yes. Mr. Mundy. He grows vegetables for the house."

"Before he moved to Pantiles, he used to have a house at Whitby. The girl's a widow, isn't she?"

"Yes."

"Thought so. Left with three young ones, wasn't she?"

"Yes."

"I see her shopping in the mornings if I'm out that way."

She held out a hand. "I'll say goodbye. We've got to meet again some time, but I'll hang it out as long as I can."

He said goodbye and drove away, acknowledging to himself that it was more comfortable to travel on pork pies and homemade biscuits than on tea and toast. His feelings were a mixture of frustration and satisfaction. He had not succeeded in recovering the three pictures, but he had made the acquaintance of Estelle, and he knew that she would stay in his mind. He felt grateful for the excuse to return—he would be doing business with Tom, but he would undoubtedly find time to call in and see Mr. Mundy and Mrs. Mallin and Estelle. He wondered how she would settle the matter of the three suitors. She could live on a prosperous farm, in a comfortable hotel—or in an ancestral mansion. He had seen, he added to himself, no desire on her part to choose any of them. The thought gave him curious pleasure.

6

There was, after all, he felt as he let himself into his rooms, no place like home. He stood on the threshold taking in the small, neat sitting room, the small, neat bedroom beyond, with a glimpse of the small, neat bathroom. Here was a way of life, he reassured himself, that offered everything a man could want.

Except space. It was, he admitted as he entered and went to the mini-bar and poured himself a drink, somewhat on the confined side. After the spaciousness of the rooms at Pantiles, he was prepared to agree that here he might possibly—if he were not so comfortable—feel contained and confined. But it was pleasant to open his cupboard-kitchen and see that here was no clutter, no unwashed crockery.

It was too late for dinner, and he was too full of pork pies to need any. He unpacked and undressed. His last waking thoughts were of two toddlers tumbling and shouting in a field, watched over by a young woman holding a baby.

He was back in his office the next day. He got a polite but not warm reception from Miss Cave, and realised that she had been expecting him to keep her in touch with the progress of his visit to the north. His report, when submitted to her, did not meet with her approval.

"I see, Mr. Netherford, no indication that you put any, as it were, pressure on her. It looks to me, from what you say here, that you simply allowed her to, shall we say, dictate her own terms."

"She wasn't in a mood to discuss anything. I was lucky to get an interview at all. She had obviously made up her mind what she was going to do. She isn't a woman who would listen to reason."

"All the same," Miss Cave stood before his desk looking down with displeasure at him in his swivel chair, "all the same, I don't think this report will satisfy our clients."

"It should. She states frankly that she's only doing this to annoy them. They'll get their pictures in the end."

"So she says. But what guarantee do we have that she'll give them up?"

"None. But I met her and as far as I could, summed her up and I feel certain that when matters move towards legal action, she'll part with the pictures. If I hadn't met Mr. Roger Brockman and his two sisters, I might not have understood her point of view—but I can well believe they treated her in the way she said they did. You weren't here when they called at the office. The are, you'll agree, a most unlovable trio."

"That may be so, but I don't think they're going to feel that this report takes them much further."

This, Edward found, was only part of what they felt. They called on him to tell him so. He listened as patiently as he could to accusations that he had been out-manoeuvred, that he had had the wool pulled over his eyes, that he had failed to—they meant, but did not say so—frighten her.

"A weak performance," summed up Millicent. "As far as I can see, we're just where we were before."

"Quite," said Audrey. "I see no point in employing a lawyer if he can't—"

"I did," Edward broke in, "as much as I could—as much as anybody could have done. The issue is not the pictures. This is a case of somebody seeking revenge for past humiliations."

"How did she expect us to treat her? As one of the family?" demanded Audrey. "Were we to watch her getting my father into her—her toils, and say nothing?"

"And now you're asking us," Millicent said angrily, "to sit and do nothing until she's decided to give back the pictures."

"We shall pursue the usual routine," Edward told them. "We shall write to her demanding the return of the pictures. We shall, if that leads nowhere, apply to the court and we shall serve her with a writ."

Which, he added to himself, she won't be there to receive. For there had been no word in his report of Mrs. Brockman's intention to leave her home and return to it only when her thirst for revenge had been assuaged. There had been nothing said about homemade pork pies and four choices of cheese. Could this, he wondered, be considered conduct unbecoming in a lawyer?

But when he looked back at that visit to Yorkshire, it was not the house near the Minster that filled his thoughts. The memory of his brief stay at the house called Pantiles seemed to become clearer as the days went by. The leisurely, casual life of its inmates

113

made his orderly, unchanging routine seem in some way pointless. Faced by Miss Cave and a file of impeccably typed papers, he realised that since his return he had had a frightening impulse to tell her there was no hurry to deal with the matter.

He received two short letters from Tom. The first told him of the progress that was being made on the rebuilding of the damaged part of the hotel. The next outlined two problems on which, he said, he would like Edward's advice as soon as he could come north and look into them. There were some scraps of other news: Mr. Mundy had won a prize at the York flower and vegetable show. Mrs. Mallin was talking of renting rooms at Robin Hood's Bay for a month, and taking Estelle and the three children.

The Brockman trio paid frequent visits to the office to find out what progress was being made towards the recovery of the pictures. Edward told them, with a satisfaction that surprised himself, that matters were at a standstill. All communications sent to Mrs. Brockman had been ignored; Edward guessed that her sister had been told not to forward letters.

It was Miss Cave who made the suggestion that he should go up to York once more.

"We're doing no good by post," she said. "If I may advise you, you'll go up there and give her one more chance of parting with those pictures. What makes you think she won't sell them?"

"That would involve her in a good deal of trouble. All she wants is—"

"I know. Nuisance value. Didn't you tell me that Mr. Parton had asked you to do some legal work for him?"

"Yes."

"Then why don't you combine the two jobs?"

"I might."

"There's nothing in the office that can't be dealt with while you're away. Did Mr. Parton say they were taking in people again at the hotel?"

"Yes. A certain number."

"Then you can stay there, and we'll be in touch." She went to the door and then turned. "Speaking of going away, may I know whether you've decided on the date of your holiday?"

He shook his head.

"Not yet. I'll let you know definitely by the end of the week."

He was finding it difficult to make up his mind about where he would take his vacation. He did not lack friends, and the friends did not lack holiday houses or chalets or villas. He had invitations to go fishing and to go sailing. He could shoot in Scotland in August; he could join a group planning a climbing holiday in Austria. He had never before had any difficulty in choosing the place and the pastime—but this year for some vague and indeterminate reason he was reluctant to make a decision.

Walking to the nearby restaurant at which he lunched habitually, he told himself that the visit to Yorkshire had unsettled him. That brief stay at the Pantiles had shown him a way of life which was alien to everything he thought of as sensible, well-ordered living. Behind or beneath the neglect of the house, the procrastination over the daily work, the disconcerting reversal of his own view of essentials and non-essentials, there had been a serenity, a satisfaction that he knew was lacking in his own life. It was what he felt to be an unreasonable conclusion, but it was one he had to accept.

At the end of the week, he told Miss Cave that he would take three weeks' holiday in September.

"Scotland?" she asked.

"No. I've had an invitation to sail to Majorca."

116

"Won't you find it too hot?"

"I might. But there'll be a lot going on."

"And when will you go up to Yorkshire?"

"I'll go up week after next."

The following week was a busy one; inside the office was a rush of work, while outside the sun shone in mocking invitation. At times like these, Edward had to remind himself that much work made much money. He told Miss Cave that he would go up to Yorkshire on the Wednesday of next week.

On Tuesday he went to lunch as usual and was given the table he preferred—one near a window overlooking the street. Sometimes he lunched alone, at other times he was joined by business associates. But he had not arranged to meet anybody on this day, and was surprised on his entrance to be approached by a waiter who informed him that a lady was awaiting him at his accustomed table.

As he crossed the room, the back view of the seated figure brought no recognition. It was not until he had reached his chair that he had a clear view and found that he was facing Mrs. Brockman.

It was a moment or two before he realised who she was. He had seen her in indoor clothing, but she was now wearing a neat navy blue coat and a small round navy blue straw hat. She was also wearing two filigree brooches and a string of white beads. Her expression was one of satisfaction.

"Thought I'd give you a surprise," she said. "Sit down. That's better. I came along at this time yesterday just to see if this was the right place—Cleeve Street, you said. I saw you come in here, so I thought I'd come today and take a chance that you'd be alone. Expecting anyone?"

"No."

"Then that's all right. I've been looking at the prices on this menu. Daylight robbery. I could get any one of these dishes up in York for half the price. What you're paying for is the frills." She waved a contemptuous hand round the flower-decked tables. "You'd do much better, and save your money, if you went along to that caffy at the end of the street. That's where I went yesterday, and had a good sandwich snack for a reasonable price."

The waiter, standing waiting for their orders, did his best to look as though he was deaf. Edward waved the menu aside.

"Avocado and sole," he said, and addressed Mrs. Brockman. "Did you say you had already ordered?"

"No. I said I was looking at the prices. You

didn't invite me, so I'll pay for my own lunch. If there's a nice steak and kidney pie," she told the waiter, "I'll have a slice."

"I'm sorry, Madam. There's no—"

"A bit of fish'll do, then. Would there be a nice bit of cod?"

"There's sole à la Florentine, Madam, with—"

"Doesn't matter what it's with, young man. Just bring me the fish."

The waiter gave place to the wine waiter.

"I'm having white wine," Edward told Mrs. Brockman. "Will you join me?"

"No, thanks. Plain water for me. Tap water, not one of those gassy bottled ones that blow you out. And now—" she leaned back in her chair as the man departed—"I'll tell you why I came."

"I hope you've come to tell me—"

"I haven't come to tell you anything. I've come to ask you how those three are holding up without their precious pictures."

"They're extremely angry, naturally."

"Naturally. Puffing and blowing the way they used to, I daresay. It was either that, or sneering. Did you tell them I was doing it on purpose?"

"No. I—"

"Well, you can let them know that my

sister's in my house, looking after it until I want to go back. The pictures aren't there. The pictures are with me. I didn't put it past those three to get into the house and walk off with them. I suppose you know that avocados are very rich? They're full of oil. It won't do your liver any good, getting through one of them a day. You haven't got any extra weight on you now, but you soon will have, I can see that. Have Audrey and Millicent got a middle-aged spread?"

"I really don't—"

"You're not the sort that would notice. They could eat—my word, they could eat. Two-course lunch, three-course dinner, and no starters like you're having to take away their appetites. Their father used just to peck at his food. You couldn't tempt him with any special dishes. Do you go out to dinner as a rule?"

"I dine out about three times a week."

"At restaurants, or your friends' houses?"

"Restaurants, as a rule."

"I thought so. There aren't many people these days who'll go to the trouble of putting a nice square meal on the table."

"On the contrary, I know people—"

"So do I. People that dish up those fancy foreign dishes, like those Indian ones that burn your tongue, or little bits of this and that called Chinese and served with chopsticks. And odds and ends on a skewer. It's a new game. Do you get into the open air much?"

"I play golf and tennis and squash."

"Golf was what Mr. Brockman played. I used to walk round with him just to watch. I never got to understanding all that jargon about birdies and whatnot."

She paused while their main course was put before them. Edward seized the chance of eliciting some information.

"I would like to know where you're staying," he said.

"I know you would. And so I'll tell you. I'm staying in Yorkshire."

"A large county, Yorkshire."

"That's right. Big enough for me to hide in."

He put down his knife and fork and studied her.

"Mrs. Brockman," he said, "are you really going to keep up this farce?"

"What farce? This fish isn't bad, only they used a bit too much butter. What farce?"

"Holding up the return of the pictures."

"That's no farce. A farce is funny, or should be, and I'm dead serious. I bet I'm not the first person that's gone on the dodge to keep what doesn't belong to them, and I daresay I won't be the last. You should have listened when I told you why I was doing it. I was getting a bit of my own back. As you don't know what living with those three was like, you can't understand what pleasure I'm getting out of doing them down. I know it can't go on for ever. What'll you do to try and find out where I am?"

"It has been known to put private detectives on to the job of finding people."

"I'd enjoy that. Trilby hats and dark glasses and black shirts and white ties, going round sniffing for footprints. Let me know when you hire them."

"I'm afraid I can't take the same casual view that you do about this affair. I—"

"There you go again. Every so often—did anyone ever tell you this? Every now and then you get a bit on the stuffy side. Pompous. You've got to watch it. You could go one way and grow into a blimp, or you could let yourself relax and let your hair down and be human. I was talking about you to those people you stayed with when you were in York. They—"

"Which people?"

"I'm just telling you. Pantiles."

"But you said—"

"I know what I said, and when I said it, it was true—I didn't know much about them. But I know more now."

"How did you—"

"That's what I mean—now you're nice and human. How did I get to know them? I work every month on the lists the tourist people keep up to date—or try to keep up to date. Hotels and other sorts of accommodation. This Pantiles was once on the list—bed and breakfast—but nobody seemed to know whether they were still in business or not—so I went there to find out. Funny set-up. Grandad, mother, daughter and three babies."

"I know."

"They told me they'd like to be scratched off the list."

"I know. They only took me in because it was an emergency. I was stranded."

"Nice babies. I didn't see much of the inside of the house, but what I did see looked as though it could do with a tidy-up. Did you say you were comfortable there?"

"I don't know whether I said so, but I was. Incidentally, I'm going up to Yorkshire tomorrow."

"Looking for me?"

"No. I'm going to do some work for Mr. Parton of—"

"I know. Cross Keys Hotel. He was lucky that fire didn't get a real hold. You going to stay there?"

"Yes."

"I might look in one day. Have your bloodhounds ready. No—you're not paying for my meal. I invited myself, I pay for myself, thank you all the same."

She paid her bill, added a minimum tip, and rose. They walked together to the door.

"Till next time," she said. "Nice to have had this chat with you."

He watched her as she walked down the street, vigorous and purposeful. Then he returned to his office feeling pleased at having received some news, however scanty, of the inmates of Pantiles.

7

Edward decided to leave in mid-morning for his drive to Yorkshire. It was a brilliant day, warm, cloudless—a perfect day, he thought, for lunching on the way at a roadhouse which served meals in a garden.

The roads were busy. He saw many cars with foreign number plates, and gathered that this was the height of the tourist season. Most of the traffic was going, like himself, northward. He lunched at one of a number of tables set under large, colourful umbrellas—an almost Continental scene, he thought, pulling his chair into the shade.

There was even more congestion on the roads in the afternoon. It slowed him down, but he was not in a hurry. He wondered how far the repairs to the Cross Keys had progressed.

He was glad to skirt York and get out of the

main stream of traffic. Driving towards Balderwick, he noted new housing estates reaching out towards the outlying villages. Soon, he reflected regretfully, the field in which Pantiles stood in such isolation would be surrounded by high-rise blocks and shops.

He drove slowly through Balderwick. As he passed the last rows of shops, he saw a feature of the village that he had not noted before: a children's playground, large, tree-shaded and well kept. There were several groups inside the wire fence—mothers with babies or young children waiting their turn on the swings and slides and roundabouts.

He had left it some distance behind when he realised that he had seen within the fence something familiar. A pram. A large pram capable of seating a baby and his two brothers. The pram from Pantiles.

He had no intention of turning back. He had come to see Tom, and he had almost reached the hotel. There was no point in going back to say a lame "Hello, how are you?" before driving on. No point—but the car was turning, seemingly of its own volition.

It stopped, or he stopped—he could not tell which—behind a short line of cars parked at the entrance. Seated at the wheel, he looked out at the lively scene. Mothers—or aunts or grandmothers—with charges ranging from babes-in-arms to shouting six-or seven-year-olds. The baby he knew as Damien was seated in the pram watching the groups with benevolent interest. Hugo and his brother were on two adjacent swings, urging their mother to push them higher and still higher.

She saw Edward, was still for a moment in surprise, and then waved. He got out of the car and stood hesitating; she could not abandon the boys and come to him, therefore he must go to her. It was not easy to reach her. Intervening were babies tumbling on the sandy floor, mothers opening packets of sandwiches and distributing them among their brood, toddlers who collided with his legs and clung there waiting to regain their balance. When he at last reached Estelle, she was laughing.

"Gulliver among the whoever-it-was," she told him.

He looked down at her. She, like the children, was wearing light cottons. She was deeply sunburnt—a smooth , even tan covering her face and neck and arms and bare legs. Her hair was taken back into a ponytail tied with narrow green ribbon.

"I saw you," he said unnecessarily, "as I drove by."

"On your way to see Tom. He was over this morning, looking forward to seeing you. He's got a room ready for you."

"So he said. He phoned last night."

"You'll have to come and see us while you're here. My mother wants to thank you for proving to us that we're not cut out for the bed and breakfast racket. Incidentally, our phone is now working."

Their exchange was banal enough, but it had, for him, a dreamlike quality. He was one man in an otherwise feminine setting. He was wearing a tie and a jacket and felt like a visitor from a colder planet. He was pushing one swing while she pushed the other. He was lifting the boys on to the slide and catching them as they reached the bottom. It all looked natural—but he did not feel at ease.

"Do you often bring the children here?" he asked.

"Hardly ever. It's usually crowded—more crowded than it is today—and there are fights all the time to get on to the swings and slides. I didn't realise how pugnacious my children were until they went pushing all the other children and hitting the ones who didn't fall down. They're stronger than I realised. I'm not popular with the other mothers."

"Then why do you come?"

"To give the children a change. Isn't this heavenly, heavenly weather? Don't you hate being cooped up in an office?"

"Sometimes. But there's work to be done."

"There were dozens of things I should have been doing today," she said. "The ironing, for a start. Turning out the kitchen cupboards. Making soup for dinner. Washing the kitchen floor. Et cetera. So what did I do?"

"You came here."

"Yes. Housework has to be done, but it has to be taught to wait until one's ready to do it. Otherwise you become what's called a slave to ceaseless labour. What would happen if you walked out of your office on a lovely morning like this, and changed into shorts and sandals and—"

"—went to play in the park? My clients would go elsewhere. The firm would collapse. I should throw my employees out of work."

"That would be a pity. See how much happier the housewife is than the careerist?"

"I begin to see. How are your mother and your grandfather?"

"Flourishing. Tom's persuaded my grandfather to grow more vegetables and sell them to the hotel. It's not a bad idea. As it is, the surplus goes to Balderwick and has to be driven from one buyer to another. Now Tom will come and fetch the fruit or vegetables—or send someone in a van—so Grandfather'll have nothing to do but dig the surplus up and load it."

"Is he able to do the extra digging?"

"So far, yes. He's very strong—like the boys." She surveyed them proudly. "They like you. That's a compliment. They're not too free with their favours."

Her mind, he noted, came back constantly to her children. She was brushing sand off them, preparatory to taking them home.

"If you hadn't brought the pram—" he began.

"You could've given us a lift home. If I hadn't brought the pram, I couldn't have brought the babies. If I'd brought a rope, you could have towed us. How long are you going to be at Tom's?"

"I've no idea. It depends on what he wants me to do."

He carried one of the boys to the pram; she had carried the other. Settling them in opposite the baby, he noted that the teddy bear it was holding was attached to a string.

"That was your idea," Estelle told him. "He's learned to throw it out and haul it up again—he's very clever."

They left the playground and walked to

the car. She stood watching him as he got in and took the wheel.

"If you come to breakfast while you're here," she said, "I'll give you a cereal—one of those that are full of nails and tintacks—and hot coffee. Do you know the poem about Conrad Katz of Kittenburg?"

"No."

"Well, his breakfast was:
'Toast cut into little bars,
Hot coffee, and some strong cigars.'
I'll substitute bacon and eggs and tomato for the cigars. Goodbye. Boys, wave goodbye to Mr. Netherford." She raised a hand. "See you—I hope."

He drove away. Nothing said—nothing of any import. But he knew that he had crossed the line dividing acquaintanceship from friendship. He had bridged the gap between being a stranger and being accepted as a friend.

On his departure from her house, he had— he now knew—wanted very much to see her again. But he had considered her way of life alien to his own. He had subjected her to a memory test and had labelled her casual to a degree, what was called feckless, careless of her house and its condition. Now his criticisms were forgotten, submerged in the one fact of her charm. She made no effort to please—but something about her had caught at his heart.

It would be better for him, he acknowledged, if he turned his car yet again—this time in the direction of home. Home? Well, back to where he had come from. She was free, but there was strong competition to persuade her to change her state. Tom loved her. Other men loved her. He was a stranger, a newcomer; to stay meant getting hurt. He had no great opinion of himself; he knew that he presented an aspect too serious, too—what was the word? Starchy. That's what he looked. It wasn't his real self, but it was the only one he was capable of showing to strangers. Nor was the starchiness only in his appearance. His employees, he knew, thought him unforthcoming, prim, unresponsive. His nature, he thought, had become as restricted as the rooms he lived in and the office he worked in. He had women friends and he had had affairs with a number of them—but they had not been affairs of the heart. And now he was allowing himself to fall into a situation in which he had never imagined he could find himself—strongly attracted to a girl who was in every way the antithesis of the kind of woman with whom he had imagined he could fall in love. She was outgoing, laughing,

132

happy-natured; if she had any interests beyond her children, he did not know of them. She had refused to let life dictate to her— she had made her own terms. And now he was within sight of Tom's hotel, and he was fated to watch Tom, and those others, try to coax her into marriage. It was not too late to go back—but he was going on.

Tom was out when he arrived at the hotel. He was shown to a comfortable room, and after unpacking, went outside and walked round the building on a tour of inspection. He had first seen the hotel when Tom had taken it over; he had seen it on fire and now he was seeing it with one side under scaffolding. He talked to some of the workmen and then wandered into the garden and sat down to tea at a small table on the terrace. He felt relaxed and cool in a short-sleeved shirt and linen trousers. He finished his tea, walked to a comfortable chair with a leg rest, and lay back with an ease that seemed to him to spring from the knowledge that the course of his life had changed direction, and he had nothing to do but follow where it led.

He was half dozing when Tom appeared beside him.

"Stay where you are," Tom said, and

dragged a long chair closer. "What's the matter with you? I've never seen you wearing a holiday aspect."

"Must be the sun. Nice to see you."

"Nice to have you here. One of the problems I mentioned to you has straightened itself out, but I'm still left with a couple. Had tea?"

"Yes, thanks."

"Then let's have a long, cool drink." He gave the order. "How're things with you?"

"Busy."

"Me, too. I might have to run up to London in connection with one of these problems you're going to tidy up. I don't fancy the trip at this time of year."

"Incidentally, I saw Estelle and the children on the way here."

"Did you go to Pantiles?"

"No. They were at the children's playground outside Balderwick."

Tom looked depressed.

"That's her life—children's playgrounds. It's becoming chronic, this devotion to her offspring. They're all she thinks about. Mother love's all very well, but it needn't turn into an obsession."

"That's apparently what she likes doing best."

"She's laying up trouble for herself. In a

few years, they won't need her."

"Not so much, perhaps. She's intelligent enough to see it coming, isn't she?"

"I suppose so. Her mother's not much help, always wrapped up in her own work."

"Estelle might marry again."

"And she might not. I told you I had rivals, didn't I?"

"Yes."

"They're still doing their best to make her see reason. I wish to God they didn't live so close to her. They're always on her doorstep." He drained his glass. "Come to that, so am I."

"I hear you're going to buy Mr. Mundy's surplus vegetables."

"Yes. He grows better quality fruit and vegetables than any of the local market gardeners. If he had to do much digging, of course, he wouldn't be able to grow any surplus, but he lets machines do the donkey work. I don't suppose you saw his rotavators when you were there?"

"No."

"By the way, didn't you mention a Mrs. Brockman once?"

"I asked you if you'd ever come across her."

"Well, I hadn't—not when you asked. But a couple of weeks ago she was at one of the tourist board meetings. She's on the committee, but I don't often go to the meetings, so I hadn't met her. I didn't speak to her—she was just pointed out to me. Efficient type. She was your client?"

"No. She's hanging on to some pictures that don't belong to her. My job is to try and get her to give them up. But she's skipped."

"Skipped?"

"She's left her house in the care of her sister, and removed herself and the pictures."

"Where to?"

"If I knew, we could serve a writ."

"What's the idea? Are the pictures valuable?"

"Moderately. Impressionists, but not top rank."

"Are you certain she went away? I have a strong feeling I caught a glimpse of her walking down the Shambles the other day."

"She's in Yorkshire. That's all I know or guess. What are these problems you've got me up here for?"

There are two. Both of the same kind. The insurance company wouldn't pay. They were demands for compensation."

"From?"

"Two baby-sitters who happened to be in the hotel on the night of the fire. Their cars were a write-off. But the cars weren't in the car park—they were both left outside the side entrance. The owners had been asked to move them, but didn't. So they want two new cars out of me. I'd like you to see both claimants. They weren't baby-sitting. They were holding up the bar until it closed. Neither of them had a current driving licence."

"I see."

"Good. I'll give you the details tomorrow. Tonight we'll enjoy ourselves. I want to take Estelle out to dinner."

"What's stopping you?"

"Three's no good. I've got to get a girl for you."

"No. Count me out."

"Why? She won't go with me. She'll only go if it's a party. You're the party."

There was no difficulty in finding a fourth. The locality, Tom said, was full of girls waiting to be taken out to dinner at short notice. This one was called Rosanna; she had been at school with Estelle, and Tom had known her for some years. It was unfortunate that she failed to do what she had been invited to do: engage Edward's attention, leaving Tom free to concentrate on Estelle. Edward did his best; he exerted himself to please—but it was clear that she regarded him merely as a fill-in, while Tom was a fixture and therefore more worth her expenditure of charm and vivacity. Edward was left to Estelle, who seemed to find the situation amusing.

"Rosanna," she said across the table, "tell us about your visit to your godmother. Was it a success?"

"How can you ask that?" Rosanna answered. "You've met her—you know what a silly old cow she is. She's just got herself a television, but we hardly ever had it on—she shunned sex, she shunned violence, she loathed pop groups, so what else was there?"

"How did you spend the evenings?"

"In what she called the lost art of conversation." Her round, somewhat vapidly pretty face was creased in distaste. "She'd start off by saying 'Let us talk', which meant that she talked about the dear old days and I thought longingly about dances and discos. *Lethal*, it was."

"Then why did you go?" Edward asked.

"Money. She's rolling, and it all comes to me if I don't do anything she disapproves of. Which is almost everything. I wanted to watch the women's gymnastic competitions, but she switched those off, too—you know why? She said she was tired of listening to the Russian national anthem. She thinks it's time I married, so she invited a succession of ghastly

138

males to dinner. All impossible, and all buried, like herself, in the most inaccessible part of Cumbria, and all desiccated. They were really *pathetic*. I came away wondering if the money was really worth it. Tom, what did you do while I was away—besides setting your hotel on fire."

"I consoled the men you left behind."

"Which particular one? Not Archie Wren?"

"No, not Archie. Archie didn't need comforting."

"I know. He's running around with one of those Standish sisters. He thought I wouldn't hear about it, but I did."

"Poison pen?" enquired Estelle.

"No. One of those well-meaning friends."

In spite of monopolising the conversation, she found time to choose the most expensive item on the menu. Tom, glancing at the bill, had a momentary fear that he had not brought enough money with him.

"Edward," he told her, "will take you home."

"No, not Edward. *You*. He doesn't know the way, and I've had too much wine to direct him, and besides that, I want to have you to myself for awhile. Estelle, d'you mind?"

"Not if Tom doesn't. Last time he took you home from a dinner, if you remember, he didn't get away until two in the morning."

"Three," corrected Tom.

"But you got away with your virtue intact," Rosanna reminded him. "Let's see if I can do better this time."

Tom saw no way, short of rudeness, to pair her with Edward. She was, he knew, acting from a mixture of mischief and spite. She knew that he was in love with Estelle, and she obviously considered that borrowing him for an evening would not alter his feelings.

He drove away with her, and Edward was left with Estelle.

"Perhaps it wasn't a good idea to ask her," she commented.

"Whose idea was it?"

"Mine. I know what she's like, but I find her amusing, and she shakes Tom up."

"He needs shaking up?"

They were walking to Edward's car. She answered with a laugh.

"I suppose he's told you that he's been in love with me for—well, ages."

"Yes. Why don't you marry him?"

"He knows why. When—*if*—I marry again, it won't be so much a husband as a father for my children."

"He'd make a good father."

"No, he wouldn't. He puts up with the three

of them. He's kind to them. He plays with them. But he doesn't *love* them."

"Aren't you asking rather a lot?"

"Of course I am." He opened the car door, and she got in and waited for him to take his place at the wheel. "I think—I've always thought that there's a big gap between a father and a stepfather. Any man I married could be a stepfather." She turned to face him. "I suppose you think that a father's irreplaceable?"

"I'd say so, yes. It's rather too much to expect a man to divide his affection between you and your children."

"That's what everyone thinks."

"Except you?"

"Except me."

"Speaking as a stranger," he stopped the car at the junction with the Balderwick road, and then drove on. "Speaking as a stranger, I'd say that you're allowing your children to get in the way of a new life for yourself."

"Do I want, do I need a new life for myself? Motherhood's regarded as a kind of fulfillment. All right, so I'm fulfilled. What else?"

"Bringing up three children might be easier if you had a husband to help you."

"And it might be more difficult. He might always remember that the children aren't his. Then I'd be what they call torn in two."

141

"Why take such a pessimistic view?"

"It's not pessimistic. It's practical, that's all."

"So you're waiting for a man to say to you: 'I love your children, please be my wife?'"

She laughed again—a sound so pleasant that he found himself thinking of bells.

"I suppose that sums it up," she said. "But if I'm waiting, wouldn't you say that I'm filling in time very nicely? I like my home, I get on well with my mother, I love my grandfather—and I've got three beautiful babies to play games with. Who could ask for more from life?"

"You will, when you fall in love."

"You're hard to convince, aren't you?"

"I'm very fond of Tom."

"And so you don't want to see him get hurt. I can understand that. But if you were not so hard to convince, I could make you see what the truth is: that being in love with me has become a very easy, comfortable state of mind. That's why I said he needs shaking up."

"I don't believe that."

"Of course you don't—but you said yourself that you're speaking as a stranger. If you lived here, you'd agree with me."

They were at Pantiles. There were lights in the hall and the kitchen.

142

"Come in and have what Tom calls a chaser," she invited.

He thanked her and accepted, and they entered the house together.

There was no sign of Mr. Mundy. Estelle's mother was seated on an easy chair, reading. She closed the book as they came in.

"Nice dinner?" she enquired.

"Expensive. Rosanna was the fourth," Estelle told her. "Did any of the children wake?"

"No. Not a peep out of any of them." She rose. "I'll follow their example and get some sleep. I've got a busy day tomorrow."

"Any order for frames?" Estelle enquired.

"Yes. Three, all in York. Goodnight. Goodnight, Mr. Netherford. It's nice to see you up here again."

She left them, and Estelle turned to Edward.

"Whisky? Cocoa?"

"That sounds nice."

"What does?"

"A nice hot cup of cocoa. I haven't had one for years."

"I have one every night."

She cleared a place for two mugs on the littered table, switched on the kettle and poured milk into a small saucepan.

"Don't let that boil over," she instructed him. "I'm going to glance at the children."

Without realising what he was doing, he went to the door of their room and stood watching. The baby was on its back, Hugo was curled into a ball and Maurice appeared to be praying with his head buried in his pillow. Estelle switched on a nightlight, made some adjustments to bedcovers and then switched off the light and led the way back to the kitchen.

"I told you to watch the milk," she said.

"I was timing it."

"Very clever. I suppose you're one of those people who can wake themselves up at pre-fixed hours?"

"No. It only works with milk."

She made the cocoa and handed him his mug.

"Let's sit in the living room," she suggested. "It isn't often I have the time, and it's a nice room. Sit down—no, not on that chair. It's got a broken spring. Try that other one. And now"—she slipped off her shoes and sat on the sofa with her feet folded under her—"now tell me about your life."

"Babyhood? Boyhood?"

"Bachelorhood." She sipped her cocoa. "I don't know why it is—I've always felt vaguely sorry for them."

"Bachelors?"

"Yes. If they're nice, I imagine that they laid their all at the feet of a cold-hearted woman and got sent empty away."

"And if they're not nice?"

"Then I think that they forswore marriage and decided to play the field. Do you play the field? I've asked you that before."

"You shouldn't ask. I wouldn't call it the field, exactly."

"Anybody in particular?"

"No. I don't seem to be the type that women go for."

"Wrong. You're the type that doesn't notice them going for you. Since I've proved to you that I lack delicacy in questioning you so closely, I can knock down the last hurdle and ask if you were ever in love."

He finished his cocoa and put down the mug before replying.

"Once or twice," he said. "At least, I thought I was, but in a curious way it wore off."

"You mean it wore out."

"No. It faded, slowly and imperceptibly."

"Did you go and see a psychiatrist?"

"Should I have done?"

"Well, it sounds to me as though the affairs had a button or two missing."

"They weren't affairs. At least, perhaps one was."

"You stun me. What was her name?"

"Maisie."

"That sounds promising. Maisie, Maisie, give me your answer, do."

"Not Daisy—Maisie. She was a Lady."

"Aren't we all?"

"I mean she had a title."

"Lady Maisie. Let me tell the rest. You had a brief, passionate affair with her and then she left you—sorry, she renounced you—to marry the marquis her parents had selected for her."

"She didn't marry. She became a nun."

Estelle studied him intently.

"There must be more to you than appears on the surface," she decided. "You mean you drove her into taking the veil?"

"I didn't drive her anywhere. She became religious and joined an Order somewhere in Kent."

"And you joined the order of bachelors?"

"I suppose you could say so. I didn't mind her going. I mean, I thought she was doing the right thing."

"To atone for doing the wrong thing. No other passionate interludes to tell me about?"

"Not that I can recall. I—what are you laughing at?"

"You. Edward U. Netherford. U for unique. More cocoa?"

146

"No, thanks. I ought to be going."

"Not before I tell you about a friend of yours who came to see me."

"A friend of mine?"

"Mrs. Brockman. She knows you bed and breakfasted here. She's something to do with the tourist board—she came to find out whether we were still on the list, and she invited herself inside to make an inspection. She didn't like what she saw."

He did not have to ask why. The evidence was all round him. It must have looked very different to the neatness and order of the house near the Minster.

"I liked her," Estelle was saying. "Nice and forthright. Is she a client of yours?"

"No. She's got something that some clients of mine want."

"Won't she hand it over?"

"At the moment, no."

"Well, she thought, and said, that this house didn't come up to the tourist board's idea of scratch. It was no use trying to explain that this is a good, docile, obedient house. When I first came to live in it, I said: Look, one of us has to have the upper hand. I'm not going to spoil you by dusting and tidying you and polishing you. That way, I'd wear myself out. You'll get—I said—the attention I want to give you, and no more. My time is to be my own and my children's—not yours. And that's how it's been ever since, and if you want to know—it's something that Tom doesn't understand and never will. He's Thomas S. P. Parton—S.P. for Spit and Polish. He ought to marry a Wren. Maybe he will, one day. And now"—she uncurled herself from the sofa—"it's time for you to get back to the hotel, or Tom will think I'm seducing you. Thank you for bringing me home."

As he drove through the dark countryside he found himself revising his opinion of cocoa as a mild drink. His head was feeling rather light, and there was a good deal of confusion in his thoughts. It seemed to him that he had been, for a short time, under a kind of spell. She was like no woman he had ever known. She laughed her way through life—and it had been, tonight, very pleasant to laugh with her.

Pleasant—and heady. He must, he decided, pull himself together—if it wasn't too late. She was Tom's. Whatever her feelings were, Tom loved her.

8

He entered the hotel to find Tom on his way up to bed.

"Thanks for taking Estelle home," he told Edward. "Did you stop for a drink?"

"Yes. Cocoa."

Tom gave a great, prolonged yawn. "Good healthy drink, cocoa," he said.

But Edward, following him up the stairs, again wondered whether this was true. Certainly it had a devastating effect on him.

He spent the next morning looking into the matters regarding which Tom had brought him up to Balderwick, and nursing the merest trace of a headache. That cocoa was certainly powerful stuff. After lunch, eaten in Tom's private dining room, Tom said that he had to go into York.

"Want to come?" he asked.

"No. What I'd like," Edward said, "is a good long walk."

"There's plenty of spare countryside for that. I tell you what: finish up at Pantiles and I'll drop by and drive you back here. Estelle might even offer us some tea."

On this they parted. Edward took a long, roundabout route, keeping to fields all the way, and at the end of it found himself within sight of Estelle's house. As he drew nearer, he saw Mr. Mundy working on the vegetable plot and Mrs. Mallin seated on a rug nearby, the three children grouped round her. A plate of jam sandwiches was being distributed between three pairs of sticky hands.

"Hello, Mr. Netherford. Come and sit down," she invited. "I'm just giving the children their tea. Estelle's out. Brian brought over a horse he's just bought, and persuaded her to go for a ride. They shouldn't be long. Is Tom meeting you here?"

"Yes. He had to go into York."

Instead of joining the tea party, Edward walked over to talk to Mr. Mundy. The old man stopped work, wiped his moist forehead and came to the gate that gave entrance to the plot.

"Nice to see you." he said. "I was just thinking of giving myself a break. Tom in York, did you say?"

"Yes. He's picking me up here."

"Then you'll want tea. We'll wait till Estelle gets back. She's riding with van Leyden. She wasn't keen on going until she saw the horse. Magnificent animal. He's a good judge of horse-flesh, is Brian. Gets it from his mother. She was a famous figure at all the hunts. They go past here sometimes, and we get a good look, but we're none of us the horsy kind. I could never afford to keep horses. Estelle had a pony for a time, but she more or less gave up riding borrowed mounts when she married. I don't think her husband was ever on a horse in his life."

They had left the vegetable plot and were seated on the grass not far from the rug. The two boys left Mrs. Mallin and joined them, Mr. Mundy fending off sticky fingers as best he could.

Edward leaned back on his hands and surveyed the landscape. No riders were in sight. He thought of them without pleasure. There was too much of this van Leyden, he thought. Shetlands for the children and magnificent animals for Estelle. Tom would arrive to find her gone. How she could accept favours from that fellow was more than he could understand. There was Tom, willing and eager to marry her, while all she did was write him off because he didn't devote himself to her children, and go floating round the country with every man who turned up with a spare horse. It was an even bet that she hadn't wanted much persuading.

The two boys had abandoned Mr. Mundy and were clambering over Edward.

"Don't let them mess you up," warned Mr. Mundy.

"Will you keep an eye on them?" Mrs. Mallin came to enquire. "I'm going indoors. I might make a start on the washing."

"Machine still out of order?" asked her father.

"Yes. The man came to have another look at the dishwasher, but he thinks it's a write-off. I would have asked him to mend the washing machine, but Estelle didn't discover it was out of order until he'd gone."

She was carrying the baby and the rug and the plate. Edward went to help her, and took the rug. They went indoors, and he saw the now-familiar array of used china and crockery.

"Washing by hand," Mrs. Mallin said, putting the baby on the floor to roam freely, "isn't going to be much fun."

"I suppose not."

"I remember being told that for every one of these machines they sold you, they ought

152

to sell you a mechanic. I didn't believe it at the time, but I do now."

She had forgotten tea, and was sorting washing into various piles. He was left to rescue the baby whenever it crawled into danger. He was now engaged in trying to climb into the round porthole entrance of the washing machine.

Lifting the baby out on its almost successful third attempt, he found himself studying the machine. There was a fixture in it which he thought might be a filter. He took a coin from his pocket, inserted it, turned and found the filter falling into his hands. He examined it with horror. Choked. Festooned with the debris of months, if not years. Strands of fibre intertwined with wool. Buttons. Hooks and eyes.

He went to the sink and began almost mechanically to clean and clear the filter. It was not easy, and as Mrs. Mallin had vanished without a word, he had to interrupt his work frequently to look under the table or behind doors to pull the baby back into view.

It was done at last. He was holding the filter under the tap when he looked up to see Estelle in the doorway.

"What on earth—" she began, and then dived to prevent the baby from pulling himself up by the tablecloth. She was too late. The cloth came off, together with all the crockery that had been on it. The baby sat, crowing with triumph, in a sea of cups and saucers. Estelle swooped to pick him up.

"Poor darling!" she crooned. "Did the horrid cloth come off? Where," she demanded, turning to Edward, "is my mother?"

"I'm here," said Mrs. Mallin, coming in from the living room. "I wasn't far away. Mr. Netherford was minding Damien and—what's all that horrid-looking stuff you're putting into the garbage bin?" she asked Edward.

"It's what came out of the filter of the washing machine. I think if you try working it, you'll find it's all right."

Together they helped Estelle to replace the crockery on the table.

"Nothing broken," Mrs. Mallin observed with satisfaction. "Mr. Netherford, I had no idea you were such a good mechanic. Where did you learn about washing machines?"

"At his mother's knee," said Estelle. "Brian's outside and he wants tea."

"So will Tom, when he comes," said her mother. "Let's wait and have it all together."

She was putting clothes into the washing machine. The filter was replaced, the appropriate knobs were turned, the current was

154

switched on. Rapt in admiration and self-congratulation, they stood for some moments watching the clothes being churned. Then Estelle turned to Edward.

"Thank you," she said. "I won't ask you to work on the dishwasher, because the man thinks it's gone beyond repair. Now you shall have some tea."

She and Mrs. Mallin prepared a tray to be carried into the garden. Edward opened a folding table and brought out easy chairs. Brian van Leyden, he noted, did precisely nothing to help. The two horses were tethered in the adjoining field where they grazed in contentment.

Tom drove up and joined the tea party but—like Edward—did not attempt to rival Brian's easy flow of conversation.

"In weather like this," he was saying, "we ought to get up some games of tennis."

"No time," said Tom tersely, his tone and attitude suggesting that he would enjoy his tea more if Brian would go and have his elsewhere. Time, Edward thought, spare time was something that this van Leyden did not appear to lack. Perhaps his farm ran itself—or it might be that there was an army of cowhands taking care of things while the boss took girls riding.

He and Tom did not stay long. After helping to carry the cups inside, they drove away, and Tom gave vent to his frustration.

"I'm getting tired of that fellow," he said. "Damned poseur, striking attitudes to show off the cut of his jodhpurs. He calls himself a farmer, but his only real interest is in horses. And, of course, Estelle."

"Does she go out much on his horses?"

"Not as much as he'd like her to. He'd like to give her one, but he knows she wouldn't accept it—apart from having nowhere to stable it. And I doubt whether she could afford its keep. She was fairly comfortably off when her husband died, but there's been something called inflation since then—and I don't think she watches the outgoings too closely."

"Does her mother make much on her picture framing?"

"I think so. Or she comes out even. But they don't eat cheaply. Old Mundy keeps them in vegetables, but they eat expensive fish—and baby foods aren't given away."

Estelle made amends for Tom's disappointment by driving over to the hotel after dinner. Tom greeted her with obvious delight, and led her into the combined drawing room and study that overlooked the gardens at the back of the building. Edward rose, pushed across a chair and wondered how soon he could use fatigue as a pretext, and leave them together. But Estelle had something to impart.

"That woman came again," she told him."The one who's on the tourist board."

"Mrs. Brockman?"

"That's it."

"You didn't by any chance find out where she was staying?"

"No. Isn't she staying in her house in York?"

"She's left it in charge of a sister, and she's—well, in a way, you could say she'd gone into hiding."

"Hiding from what?"

"Me. She's got three pictures that some clients of mine want. In fact, they own them."

"And she doesn't want to give them up?"

"Not yet. She's getting her own back for past disfavours."

"She the one you told me had skipped?" Tom asked.

"Yes."

Tom turned to Estelle.

"Why did she go and see you?"

"I think she wanted to know how long Edward was staying up here. As I didn't know, she had to go away empty. She knew he was at this hotel—why didn't she come here and ask him?"

"I've no idea."

"And why did she think I'd know your plans?" she asked Edward.

"I think I can answer that," Tom said. "I was waiting to cross a road, and she drove by in a car which I think was made from the remains of the Ark. She stopped, leaned out, asked whether Edward was with me, and I said I was meeting him at Pantiles. Perhaps she expected him to be there."

"He wasn't," said Estelle. "She didn't stay long, but she was a terrific success with Hugo and Maurice. She taught them to play hopscotch. I don't know who looked funniest—she or the boys."

"If she visits you again, perhaps you could find out where she's staying," Edward suggested.

"She can't be far away. She came in the car that Tom saw. It's going to fall apart any moment now. She told me she only uses it for short distances."

"Speaking of your plans," Tom asked Edward, "where are you going to spend your holiday?"

"I don't know. I told my secretary I might go sailing in September."

"Why not come up here?" Tom suggested.

"That doesn't sound very exciting," Estelle commented. "He's probably going to Kashmir or Samarkand."

"Well, if he's not," Tom said, "He could do worse than a vacation up here. I'll have more time, the repairs will all be done, there's a nearby golfcourse and I can lay on tennis and squash courts and a swimming pool. I'd suggest teaming up and going with you to one of those places Estelle mentioned, but I don't want to leave this hotel till I've got it running as it used to run. Think it over."

Edward promised that he would, and rose to say goodnight.

"It's early yet," demurred Tom.

"I know. But that was a long walk."

In his room, he undressed and got into bed and lay thinking of them. Perhaps Tom would—yet again—ask her to marry him, and she might, this time, say yes. And in the meantime he himself would have to occupy his time in keeping out of their way and mending washing machines.

His light was still on when Tom came upstairs. He stopped to knock on the door, and on Edward's answering, put his head in.

"Forgot to tell you," he said. "Didn't you mention three missing or purloined pictures?"

"Yes. At least, Mrs. Brockman is hanging on to them."

"Well, I dropped into Anthony Brewster's shop—if you can demean it by calling it a shop—to pay a bill. He happened to mention that a woman—a woman he didn't know—had brought in three pictures to be valued."

"Did he say what they were?"

"No, and I was in a hurry and didn't stop to ask. But you might care to follow it up."

"I will. Thanks."

"D'you think they're the pictures you're after?"

"I'll tell you when I've talked to Brewster."

"Be odd if there was a connection. I hear you mended a washing machine."

"Pure luck. I saw what looked like a filter, and filters have a way of jamming the works. So I cleaned it."

"If you hadn't, I wonder how long they would have gone on doing the washing by hand? See what you can achieve with the dishwasher. What d'you think of van Leyden?"

"A bit too pleased with himself."

"He's a damned nuisance."

"Why don't you buy a string of horses and go into competition?"

"Because I'm short of time. This place takes all I've got. That's why I have to give other fellows a free hand to hang round Estelle. I wish I thought I was making progress. Well, I won't keep you up. Goodnight. Incidentally, I've got to spend some time in York tomorrow. Want to come?"

"No thanks. I'll go in on my own and have a word with Brewster about those pictures."

"Would you like me to fix you up with a round of golf in the afternoon?"

"No. I enjoyed that walk today—I'd like to do it again. Goodnight."

9

Edward drove to York early the following morning, and after some wrong turnings, found himself outside the double-fronted showroom owned by Anthony Brewster. The single name—Brewster—was displayed in discreet lettering, and both windows were filled with works of art—china, silver, figurines, pictures—protected by wire mesh.

He had to go some distance before he could park the car. Then he walked back, pushed open the elegant glass-and-chrome door, and entered. The interior was bright from the light of the windows, but at the back were shadowy offices. There were two well-dressed assistants—girls who could have graced the members' enclosure at Ascot. To one of these, when she offered to assist him, he said that he would like to see Mr. Brewster on some private business. She entered one of the offices,

162

and from it emerged the man Edward had come to see.

The words 'Nice place you've got here' almost came to Edward's lips, but he suppressed them. Anthony spoke first.

"I've met you before," he said. "At Pantiles."

"Yes. I'm staying at the Cross Keys. Last night Tom mentioned that a woman had come in with three pictures and asked you to value them."

"That's right. I thought they were for sale. All she wanted was a valuation. I naturally assumed that she wanted to sell them, so I did my best to give her a fair figure. Whereupon she thanked me and said that was all she'd wanted. Damned nerve, coming in here and using me as a valuer without any intention of selling. Are you interested in the pictures, or in the woman who brought them in?"

"Both."

"She left no name. The pictures were minor Impressionists. I told her she wouldn't get more than twenty thousand pounds apiece. She'd probably get less than that from most dealers."

"What did she look like?"

"Provincial but prosperous. Stoutish, neatly turned out, Yorkshire accent. I would have liked to know who she was, but didn't succeed in getting either a name or an address out of her. Neither of my assistants have ever seen her before."

"The pictures—"

Anthony described them, but Edward was already certain that they were the property of the Brockman trio. He thanked the other man and prepared to depart.

"How are the hotel repairs getting on?" Anthony asked.

"More or less done. The scaffolding's to come down today."

"I hope Tom's business picks up. It will in time, of course—the place is well-known and was very seldom anything but full. How long have you known him?"

"Tom? We were at school together. We've been friends ever since. Sorry to have taken up your time."

"What's your interest in the pictures?"

"They belong to clients of mine. Mrs. Brockman—the woman who brought them in here—decided to hang on to them for a while."

"Well, I don't want to dishearten you, but from the little I saw of her, I'd say she'd be hard to coerce. I wish you luck."

"Thanks."

Walking to his car, Edward decided on an

impulse to drive to the house near the Minster and see just who was in residence. He did not think he would find out anything about Mrs. Brockman's whereabouts, but there was a slender chance that the sister—if she was living in the house—might tell him something.

The woman who answered the door was like enough to Mrs. Brockman to make it more than likely they were sisters.

"I came," he told her, "to see if Mrs. Brockman was still here."

She opened the door wider.

"Come in," she invited. "I'm her sister. My name's Mrs. Durham. Mrs. Durham of Durham, I always tell people."

She was stouter than her sister, and her vowels sounded broader. She looked about fifty, and had a sensible air and manner, but she lacked the look of firmness or obstinacy that was so apparent in Mrs. Brockman. She led him into the drawing room that he had seen before.

"Sit down," she said. "My sister said she thought you might drop in—to see if she's been speaking the truth about going away. But she wasn't lying. She went. She wouldn't tell me where."

"I presume she took the pictures with her."

"That she did. And a fine business we had

getting them down off the wall and packing them and getting them into her car."

"Did she give you any idea as to when she'd return?"

"No. But she won't hurry." She paused. "I'll tell you something, Mr. Netherfold. She—"

"Ford. Netherford."

"My sister said Nettlefold. Now you've got me all mixed up."

"You were saying—?"

"I was going to tell you that this hanging on to something that doesn't belong to her—it's not like her. She's doing it to get her own back."

"I know."

"You don't know what she went through with those daughters of Mr. Brockman. The son wasn't so bad—but the other two were past everything. My sister wouldn't have stood it for half a day if it hadn't been for the old man. He took a fancy to her, right from the start, and when his children—if you can call them children, the age they are—when they saw the way things were going, they did all they could to put the old man against her. Wicked, they were."

"I was never told the full story."

"Well, you wouldn't hear it from them,

166

would you? Not likely. And my sister never told me the whole of it. She should never have gone to work for them. I told her so at the time. I said to her: 'Why not retire? You've got a good home.' You know this house is hers, don't you? I said: 'You've got a good home, and enough money to keep you in comfort.' But she'd got restless after turning down a number of jobs. She wanted to be up and doing. And this job sounded just what she wanted—old man, middle-aged son, two middle-aged daughters, nice house—"

"And other servants."

"That's right. Her job was to engage them—cook, parlour-maid, housemaid. She didn't stop to wonder why the previous lot had all left the job, one after the other. She went for an interview. One of the daughters let her in, polite as you please, and took her to the old man's study, and it was him did the interviewing. She liked him from the start. She said he had a kind of lost look. So she took the job and engaged the other servants, but none of them would stay long. You can't treat servants today in that uppity way the two daughters did. My sister had the house and the cooking on her hands, but she got dailies to help her, and things went along all right until the old man's wife died and he began to depend on her, and showed he'd got fond of her. Then the three—the son and the daughters—decided to get rid of her, but their father wouldn't hear of it. They did every dirty thing they could— they even hid bits of jewellery and silver and said she'd taken them, but the old man was too sharp to be taken in. It ended with him telling my sister he wanted to marry her, and they got married and he brought her up to this house and they were as happy as larks, right up to the time he died. He hadn't left anything to her in his Will—that was all fixed before they left London—but there were these three pictures he was to have for his lifetime, and then they were to go to his children. And don't you fear—my sister's straight as straight, and they'll get them in the end, but I've told you all this to explain that she feels it's her due to get her own back on them. They think a lot of those pictures. Myself, I can't see that they're all that good. They look kind of smudgy to me—but there it is. My sister's hanging on to them."

"You've no idea where she is now?"

"No, and if I knew I wouldn't tell you. She hasn't gone far. Friends we know have seen her in York from time to time, but where she's hidden those pictures, I can't tell you."

He saw no point in prolonging the visit. It

was not far off lunch time, but he did not think that she would lead him to the dining room and ask him to share a feast, as her sister had done. He thanked her and drove away, trying to make up his mind whether to go back to the hotel for lunch, or go to a restaurant in York.

And then he drove past a line of people waiting for a bus, and among them was Estelle.

He came to an abrupt halt and reversed, but she was already coming to meet him. She spoke through the window.

"Going my way?"

"If I wasn't before, I am now." He was beside her, opening the door. "Get in."

He went back to the driver's seat, and she told him why she was in York.

"I made up my mind to come and say some rude words to the dishwasher people. I got tired of telephoning and getting put off with promises. I was going to drive myself, but Tom arrived to say he'd been called to York and wouldn't be back until the evening. I asked him to drop me at the dishwasher's."

"How did you plan to get back?"

"Bus. A heavenly ride in a lovely car one way, humble bus the other. And now here you are to take me home."

He summoned his courage.

"I was just going to have lunch. I suppose I couldn't persuade you to join me?"

"And what becomes of my babies?"

"I presume you left your mother in charge?"

"My mother *and* my grandfather. I feel safer when they're both on the job. So yes, thank you, I'd love to have lunch with you."

"Good. You know this city better than I do. Where would you suggest going?"

"Have you ever been to Merlin's?"

"No. Is it old, new?"

"Old building, new restaurant—just the other side of Bootham Bar. Tom took me there once, because the food was, as he said, always superlative. Do you like seafood?"

"In moderation, yes."

"That sounds just like you. In moderation. I have a feeling it's the rule you live by. And why not? In moderation. I remember my husband used to say that moderation was the secret of happiness. Of course it isn't. I told him so. Turn left at the lights."

He turned left. The restaurant was at the end of a narrow street, but there was a parking space close by. Here he left the car.

"Seventeenth century," she told him as they walked together to the small, timbered building. "They say one of Charles the Second's mistresses lived in it once, but there's no actual proof."

170

"It looks rather small for a King's mistress."

"He might have run out of palaces to house them in. I hope we can get a table looking out on to the mini-garden at the back. The owner keeps one for himself, but if you mention Tom's name, he'll let us have it."

The mention of Tom's name secured them the table. When they had taken their places and had been left to study the menu, Edward asked what connection Tom had with the restaurant.

"Tom's chef started the place. He was with Tom's father for years, and Tom inherited him. Then he brought his son over from Orleans, and now the son's Tom's chef and his father's making a fortune running this restaurant. His wife came over with the son; she works here as pastry cook. Can I begin with avocado? They do a wonderful fish soup, if you like soup."

"No soup. Cold salmon, I think."

"Good idea. Me, too."

"Mussels to start off with."

He chose the wine, and it proved to be the right degree of coolness. She sipped it appreciatively.

"Tom thinks I haven't a bad nose for wine," she said. "It's a case of ignorance triumphing over experience, he says."

171

It was as well, Edward thought, that Tom's name figured in the conversation. It kept a rein on his feelings, which were threatening to get the better of him. The room was small, intimate. The service was impeccable, the atmosphere one of quiet luxury. A table overlooking a tiny colourful garden, a girl with fair, free-flowing hair and a wide, smiling mouth . . .

She did not look older or younger than her age, which by now he knew to be twenty-four. Her eyes were clear, her skin flawless. She had rounded, tanned arms and stockingless, tanned, beautiful legs. She was casual, unselfconscious, interested in everything about her—and interested, too, in him.

"I was thinking about you at the bus stop," she told him. "I wondered what your daily routine was. How do you fill in all the hours that millions of other people have to spend in preparing meals and washing clothes and ironing clothes and so on and on? Do you ever cook a meal for yourself?"

"Cook, no. But if I don't feel like going out, I make sandwiches and coffee."

"Frozen food ready to put into the oven?"

"No."

"Then you never invite friends to have a meal in your rooms?"

"Friends like Tom, yes. When he comes to London, he and I talk and eat sandwiches and drink beer."

"And women?"

"I take them out. Most women I know wouldn't settle for beer and sandwiches."

"If they were in love with you, they wouldn't know what they were eating. Or where."

"Then let's say they're not in love with me."

She put down her fork and spoke insistently.

"Not even one?"

"At the moment, no."

"Tom says you don't go after women, but women run after you. Don't you ever let them catch you up?"

He laughed, and she looked across the table with a puzzled expression.

"Why don't you do that more often?" she asked.

"Do what?"

"Laugh. You smile when there's anything to smile at, but you don't often laugh right out as you just did. It made you warm and friendly and—and human. It cut across the barrier you seem to have put up between you and the stronger emotions. Do you know there's a barrier?"

"Wouldn't shyness make a kind of barrier?"

"I suppose so. But Tony Brewster said that as soon as he met you, he said 'lawyer' to himself. You were in his showroom this morning, weren't you?"

"Yes. Someone had taken those three pictures to him and asked him to value them. I'd like to have a valuation of his stock-in-trade."

"All of it chosen by himself. He spends a lot of his time going round the Middle East, combing the markets. He's very well known. If you see a queue outside the shop, they're not people waiting to get in—they're just waiting for a Royal Personage to come out."

"Did he inherit the shop?"

"No. At least, not exactly. An uncle of his owned it and wanted to give it up. It was to go to Tony when he died, but he said he didn't want to die in harness, so he handed it over to Tony in return for an undertaking that Tony would support him in comfort for the rest of his life. Which Tony did—he only died four years ago. In Wales. He wasn't Welsh, but he went very Welsh towards the end— learned to speak the language, and practised singing, that kind of thing. Are you English?"

"Yes. My mother was a Jersey woman."

"But your parents didn't live to bring you up?"

"No. I was brought up by a rather religious aunt. She used to design Christmas cards for the young—kind of illuminated texts. She said it was the young who needed guidance."

"Catch 'em young. That was what the Druids did, isn't it? Or was it the Jesuits? Nobody guided me. My grandfather teetered on the edge of Roman Catholicism but never actually went over. My mother is an all-roads-lead-to-Heaven believer. So I was left to find my own road. Isn't this salmon heavenly?"

"It's extremely good."

"Sorry. It's extremely good. Speaking of Druids, they were a nasty lot on the whole, weren't they? Human sacrifice, no less. No wonder the Romans wiped them out."

"The Romans eradicated them because they had too much political power."

"A happy band, I remember thinking when I learned about them at school. Free from taxes, tribal obligation and conscription."

"Yes. Owing allegiance only to the Archdruid."

"I wrote a prize essay about them but I've forgotten most of it. There wasn't much to write about their religion."

"They believed in the immortality of the soul. They were teachers and judges of Celtic society."

"And no appeals allowed from their sentences. Tom went with me to a fancy dress dance dressed as a Druid, but he wasn't much of a success. Everyone thought he was an Arab. I think he got the headdress wrong."

"What were you dressed as?"

"A female Druid. That didn't win a prize, either. Do you go to many dances?"

"Not nowadays. I used to when I was younger."

"I used to go to university get-togethers in London with my husband. That was before the babies came."

"I thought babies meant an interval, and not a complete changeover."

"In my case, they meant a changeover. If you think of it, it's a pretty demanding job. That is, it's demanding if you take it seriously."

"Which you do."

"Does it show?"

"Very clearly. What happens when they leave you?"

"All I want to do is cover the time they're at the helpless stage—when they're totally dependent. When they can dress themselves, put themselves to bed, walk down a safe street alone—I'll know the first part of the job is done. I hope they'll enjoy going to school as much as I did."

"Hugo and Maurice and Damien. Are they family names?"

"No. Picked out of a hat. Where do the Netherfords come from? You're the first one I've met."

"It's a common name in Cambridgeshire."

Their main course plates had been removed. A waiter was hovering with the dessert trolley. She gave it an attentive survey.

"Something chocolatey," she told the waiter. "Those round things over there. And could I have a peach too?"

She was given a generous helping of each. Edward resisted all the waiter's blandishments, and ordered two coffees. Then he sat watching as she ate with schoolgirlish enjoyment.

"How do you keep your elegant figure?" he asked her.

"By not lunching at the Merlin. Have you enjoyed the food?"

"The food, and the wine—and the company," he managed to say. Her eyes widened.

"So shy, but so gallant," she commented.

"I'd like to take you out again if you ever came to London."

"It's like York in a way, isn't it? So much history. So much to look at, so many places to visit and to study."

"Do you know it well?"

"We were taken twice a term on what went down on the school bill as cultural expeditions. Private bus, two accompanying teachers, beans on toast at a respectable café, and kindly pay attention or you won't be able to do your essay tomorrow. We were allowed to sing folk songs on the journey back to York. Nowadays I sing them to the boys if they can't sleep. Are you in a hurry to get back?"

"No. Are you?"

"I haven't got long—but long enough to do a sort of detour. How do we know how long this gorgeous weather is going to last?"

They took the return journey slowly, and she showed Edward narrow, green country lanes that he had never before explored.

"Doesn't this make you want to sing about the greenwood?" she asked.

"I can't sing."

"You can try."

"In summer time when flowers do spring And birds sit on each tree . . ." he essayed.

There was a pause.

"You do the driving," she decided. "I'll do the singing."

"You've got a nice voice."

"It's better than nice. I used to sing all the solos in Chapel. Hark hark the lark. You know, I think I was born under a lucky star. All the men I know have such heavenly cars. Brian's is the smoothest, but it's also the showiest. I think it must have been designed for an oil sheik. Do you like him?"

"Van Leyden? Since you ask, no."

"You mustn't be put off by his manner. Lots of people are as . . . as vain as he is; they're just better at hiding it, that's all. Anthony Brewster's no shrinking violet."

"You've got the brightest star: Tom. What do the others matter? It's hard for me, knowing Tom as well as I do, to understand why any woman doesn't seize him while he's available."

"You've missed the turning to Balderwick."

He reversed and made a U-turn. The road back. The road back to her children and her parent and grandparent and all her domestic preoccupations.

"If you come to London," he said, "will you let me know?"

"Of course. I'd like to see you in your bachelor hideout. Whereabouts is it?"

"Cicero Mansions. Chiswick."

"With windows overlooking Father Thames."

"Only two windows on the river side."

They were driving beside her river. She

looked out at it with a smile.

"Two different ways of life," she said. "Your river, wide and deep and flowing swiftly. And my river—this sluggish little stream choked by weeds and greenery. The city of London—the Vale of York. A bachelor without ties, a mother with three prize infants. They are prize infants, wouldn't you say?"

"They're a very healthy trio."

"Ah—moderation. I wish I could believe that one day you'll burst your shirt buttons getting enthusiastic about something. Or someone."

"I'll keep you informed."

They were home. Mrs. Mallin gave a sigh of relief, handed over her charges and went into the building in which she did her picture framing. Mr.Mundy was dozing in his deck-chair.

"I ought to do some baking," Estelle said, and turned to Edward. "Could I leave the children with you for a little while?"

He looked apprehensive.

"To . . . to look after, you mean?"

"Just to keep an eye on. I'd suggest a short walk, but the weather's a bit changeable. It's all right at the moment. If you all sat on a rug under a tree, you could tell them a story."

"Story?"

180

"Yes. Story. You know—Snow White and the dwarfs, that kind of thing."

She took the children into the garden. The baby lay contentedly in its canvas cot. Hugo and Maurice sat on the rug looking expectant. Mr. Netherford, they had been informed, was going to tell them a story.

There was silence when Estelle went indoors. The baby continued to play with its toes. Edward sat with his back against the tree and the two boys waited.

"What sort of story?" Hugo asked at last.

Edward searched his mind for stories, and found none. He had no memory of anybody telling him nursery stories. The children of his friends were past the age at which nursery tales interested them. Snow White? An apple came into it—and all the dwarfs had names which he had long forgotten, if he had ever known them.

"Not Snow White," Hugo said. "Tell a new story. About animals."

"Bears," added Maurice. "Not teddy bears."

"Lion." Hugo spread his arms wide. "A great, hooje lion."

"What roars," said Maurice.

"I don't know any stories about lions," Edward told them. "I know one abut a hen."

"No."

"No. Not hen. Lion."

Edward began with a confidence which promptly left him as he uttered the first sentence.

"Once upon a time there was a lion." Pause.

"And then what?" asked Hugo.

"Was he a lion in a zoo?" suggested Maurice.

"No."

So much Edward was certain of. No lions in zoos. A free-ranging lion.

"Not in a zoo," he said. "This lion was . . . he lived in a forest."

"Forest?" repeated Maurice in an enquiring tone.

"Lotsa trees," said Hugo. "Where was the forest?"

"It was . . . well, I'm not quite sure exactly where it was, but it was near some houses—a sort of nice village where people lived."

The two listeners sensed that this was a beginning.

"And then what?" Maurice asked.

"Houses. A sort of village, as I said. There were fathers and mothers and children. A great many children. They used to play every day—after they'd come home from school, or all day if they didn't go to school—and they stayed close to their houses and gardens because one of the mothers said she had once seen a lion in the forest. So the children were told they mustn't go too near the forest, just in case."

"Just in case the lion ate them?" Hugo asked.

"Yes, something like that. But the lion that the mother had seen had been a very small lion."

Another pause. The background was set— what came next?

"A very small lion. And this lion, because he was very small, liked to watch all the small children playing outside the forest. He began to learn all their names, and he got to know which houses they lived in, and he liked them more and more, and began to come nearer and nearer to watch them playing. But one day, some mothers saw him and got frightened and told him to go away. He went, not far, because he couldn't bear to leave all the children he liked so much—but he was careful to hide behind the trees so that nobody would see him."

"Where was his mother and father?" asked Maurice.

"They lived in the forest, but they never came near the houses, and they would have been worried if they'd known that the baby lion had got so near them—but they didn't know, because he just said he was going for a walk, and then went to watch the children. But the children never went near him—their mothers had told them to keep away. There was only one little boy—his name was Robert—who wasn't in the least afraid of the baby lion, and went quite near him—not near enough to stroke him, but near enough to talk to him. And the lion answered him, but of course he couldn't talk, he could only roar, and when he roared, even if it was only a baby roar, it made a frightening noise."

This was going rather well, he thought. There wasn't much art in telling stories, once you got a start. The two boys were listening with absorbed interest. Chapter two.

"But one day, the mothers took a picnic into the forest, and a lot of children went with them, and they had a lovely time eating nice things and playing among the trees. And then when it began to get dark, they all packed up the picnic things and went home. And when they got home, Robert's mother began to cry, because she had noticed that Robert hadn't come home with the others. And then everyone got very frightened, because it was quite dark, and Robert didn't have a torch, and they knew he wouldn't be able to find his way home without one."

"And so?" Maurice asked.

"And so all the fathers got together and said they would go into the forest with lamps and look for Robert. And one of the fathers said they had better take their guns with them, in case they met any lions."

"Would they shoot them?" Hugo asked.

"Well . . . they wouldn't want to. It would all depend on whether the lions were friendly or not. So all the fathers set off, and they called Robert's name as they went, and they walked deeper and deeper into the forest looking for him. And suddenly Robert's father put up his hand and said to the other fathers: 'Wait. I see something.'

"They all stopped and tried to see what he had seen. Presently they could make out Robert, lying asleep on a bed of leaves, and beside him, close to him so as to keep him warm, was the baby lion.

"'Put down your guns,' Robert's father said. 'Robert is in no danger.'

"'But that's a lion!' the other fathers said. 'It may only be a baby lion, but it's a lion just the same, and it's close to Robert and may hurt him.'

"'Can't you see what he's doing?' Robert's

father said. 'He's watching over Robert, seeing he doesn't come to any harm. He's keeping him warm. He's guarding him.'

"By this time, the baby lion had got up, and didn't move away when all the fathers came closer to see him. They woke Robert up, and Robert said in a frightened voice, 'You didn't hurt the lion, did you?' and his father said, 'No.'

"Robert was stroking the baby lion.

"'He saved me,' he told the fathers. 'I was going deeper and deeper into the forest, but he made me come back here, because this is the place we had our picnic, and he knew that it was here that you'd all come and look for me.'"

A fine climax, thought the narrator. Really, there was nothing to worry about. Next time he was asked to amuse children with stories, he would be able to call on this untapped well. How extraordinary that he had never suspected he had this gift. But he must wind up the thing.

"And they all went home, but after that, when the baby lion came to watch the children playing, nobody shooed him away. When he grew bigger, he didn't come any more, but none of the children ever forgot him."

The end. Perhaps a bit lame, that last bit,

but there were no complaints from the listeners. In fact—a slight uneasiness gripped him—there was no sound of any kind from the listeners. He peered down at the two heads leaning against his arms. No sound, and no movement. Utter stillness. Even the baby's legs were no longer waving in the air.

From the door of the house, an amused voice reached him.

"Congratulations. Nobody's ever succeeded in doing that before."

He eased himself away from the two boys, and stood up.

"Nobody's ever what?"

He was going over to join her. She was wearing an apron, and her arms were white with flour.

"Nobody's ever sent them off to sleep. I didn't know you were a story-telling genius."

"Neither did I. Want any help with the cake-making?"

"No. Come in and watch. I've done most of it."

He went inside, sat on a chair and watched while she brushed flour off the table. An appetising smell came from the oven.

She stopped for a moment to study him, and then spoke in a musing tone.

"I can't decide," she said, "about whether

you'll come back or not. Whether we'll meet again. At times I feel we will, and then again, I feel you're going for good."

That was true enough, he thought. He was going for Tom's good.

He was silent. She finished clearing away the mixing bowl and flour and then glanced out of the window.

"Children awake," she announced.

"Shall I bring them in?"

"No. My mother's bringing them."

They came in and watched with breathless interest the cakes and scones being taken out of the oven and placed on a wire tray. Then the telephone rang, and Mrs. Mallin answered it. There was a pause, and then she gave a cry of surprise. Thereafter, the warmth and politeness of her words were a ludicrous contrast to the dismay that overspread her countenance.

"Oh really? How nice. Yes, of course, *do* drop in. We shall love seeing you."

"*Who?*" whispered Estelle. Mrs. Mallin put up a warning hand and continued the conversation. "Of course. How long are you going to be in York? Only two days? What a pity . . . yes, do bring her with you. We should like to see her. Well, goodbye for the moment. We'll look out for you in—what? Let's say half an hour."

She replaced the receiver and faced Estelle.

"Miss Curtis," she groaned.

"Oh my God. And who else?"

"Her sister. I'd forgotten she had a sister. I thought they were safely in Guernsey. That's where Miss Curtis went when she retired. But they're in Yorkshire, driving round, dropping in—she said—to say how d'you do to old friends."

Estelle turned and spoke hurriedly to Edward.

"My old headmistress," she explained. "Let's get started."

She had already embarked on a frenzied bout of tidying. Helped by her mother, both working in grim silence, they hurried round opening cupboards, pushing the nearest articles into them and closing them again. Mrs. Mallin went into the living room and began pushing books, knitting, toys and miscellaneous articles out of sight behind chairs. Estelle had got out the vacuum cleaner. She thrust the handle into Edward's hands and gave a curt order.

"Hurry. And only where it shows."

He found himself pushing the machine to and fro in the kitchen and the living room. Mrs. Mallin, breathless from haste, provided a jerky explanation.

"Mania for tidiness. And she always gives little or no notice in the hope of finding us in a mess. Estelle was the school's neatest pupil, and her ex-headmistress tells people what a wonderful housewife she's become." She handed him a duster. "Just dust round things—don't lift them up. But be careful—she won't miss a thing."

At the end of fifteen minutes, the rooms looked models of tidiness. Estelle went round on a tour of inspection.

"It'll do," she pronounced. "Thanks, both of you. Mother, will you go and warn Grandad, and then change the children's clothes?"

Mrs. Mallin hurried the children into their room. Estelle went to tidy herself and Edward was left alone to look round the rooms with an ex-headmistress's eye. He thought uneasily that if someone made a mistake and opened one of the over-full cupboards, there would be a cascade of articles. Nice rooms, he decided, now that one could really see them.

The visitors drove up in a small station wagon and were welcomed at the front door by Mr. Mundy, Mrs. Mallin, Estelle and the children. Edward was left in the living room. It was some time before they joined him, for there were children to be admired, Mrs. Mallin congratulated on the widespread success of her picture-framing, and Mr. Mundy assured that he didn't look a day older than he had done when last they saw him. Then they came in and Mrs. Mallin introduced Edward. He was, he learned, a friend who had stayed with them for a little while.

"He was to have stayed at Tom Parton's hotel," she told Miss Curtis. "You know there was a fire there?"

"Indeed, yes. Several people wrote to tell us about it."

To Edward she looked exactly as he had imagined a successful retired Headmistress would look—tall, slender, well-dressed, with a voice which, though low, had something commanding about it. Her skin was smooth, her nose Roman, her manner just short of patronising.

Her sister, introduced to him as Mrs. Winch, was by contrast, he considered, something of a let-down, being extremely plain, extremely stout and brusque to the point of rudeness. Her first remark was made after a disparaging glance out of doors.

"Ever tried growing any flowers?"

Mr. Mundy might have answered this, but he had been edging towards the door and now, with a muttered sentence about getting back to work, made his escape.

"We did make some attempts at a garden," Mrs. Mallin said, "but none of us had the time to give to it."

"I should've thought your father could have produced a bloom or two. Not much more trouble, when you come to think of it, to stick in a lily than to plant a lettuce. Couldn't live without flowers, myself."

Edward looked up at the hanging greenery in the hope of drawing her attention to it, but she gave it no more than a contemptuous glance.

"Colour's what I like," she said. "Roses, lilac, delphiniums, larkspur. Colour. Don't understand how people with room to grow them don't make an effort."

"I remember how beautifully Estelle used to do the flower arrangements in the assembly hall and in my study." This was Miss Curtis pouring on oil. "So artistic. What beautiful grounds the school had! I found it very hard to leave them when I retired."

"Do you like living in Guernsey?" Edward asked her.

"Yes and no. We—"

"Chiefly no," broke in Mrs. Winch. "All right in winter, but stuffed with tourists all through the summer. Pests."

"My sister used to travel a good deal when

her husband was alive," Miss Curtis said. "Always going off to exotic places. I used to try and get her to lecture on some of the wonders she had seen, but—"

"Not to giggling girls," said Mrs. Winch. "Waste of time."

"Such a pity. You're so splendid at addressing meetings," her sister told her.

Edward could believe this. That expanse of bosom alone would be enough to intimidate any audience. He wondered what her husband had done besides going to exotic places. On second thoughts perhaps she had gone alone.

As if she had read his thoughts, Miss Curtis said that the late Mr. Winch had been a mining engineer.

"Explorer on the side," Mrs. Winch added. "I used to ask him what was the use of seeing all those places if he didn't write about them. That's what he should have done, but one of his greatest faults was that he couldn't apply himself. Always on the move, no time to make any useful notes that I might have published later."

Edward was summoning his courage to ask why she hadn't made any notes herself, but at this point, Estelle suggested tea.

The weather had been considered too uncertain to have tea out of doors. The table was laid in the living room, and the chairs of the three children drawn up to it. Estelle was sending nervous glances at the cupboards, and Edward knew that she was trying to remember which one the clean china was in. He went into the kitchen and open the right one. Estelle followed him.

"Thanks," she said. "Will you carry trays?"

He helped her while Mrs. Mallin lifted the children into their places and settled the visitors. When the cakes were brought in, Hugo looked at them with displeasure.

"That chocolate one is Maurice's," he told the visitors. "And the other one is mine. Mummy made them specially for us."

"Well, you won't mind sharing them with us, will you?" Miss Curtis asked in a teasing tone.

"You can have a little bit, but not much," he answered. "It's got to last till next baking day."

"Share and share alike," said Estelle.

"Don't believe in rich cakes for children," Mrs. Winch said. "Good bread and butter's what they should have."

"Not all the time?" Hugo suggested.

"Most of the time."

The meal, begun on this note, was not a success. The children seemed to be on their worst behaviour, and everybody was glad when the ordeal was over and the visitors said they must hurry away. They were seen off, Mr. Mundy waving from the vegetable patch, and Estelle and Mrs. Mallin gave a sigh of relief.

"Thank heaven they live a long way away," Mrs. Mallin said. "Just imagine if they lived nearer and could drop in frequently."

"We'd probably learn to be tidy," Estelle said. "I'm glad they didn't stay long. I can't take too much of that sister." She looked at Edward. "I suppose," she challenged him, "you think I went to a lot of trouble for nothing?"

"Why did you?"

"Because . . ." she stopped and frowned. "To tell you the truth, I don't quite know why. It began the first time she came here—she retired from the school not long after I left it. I'd let the house go, and I suddenly saw it as she'd see it—a deplorable falling of standards in a girl who'd once taken prizes for good housekeeping. So, the first time she came, I did a lightning clear-up—and on subsequent visits I suppose it became a habit. Fortunately, she doesn't come to Yorkshire more than once a year."

"Does she live with the sister who came with her?"

"No. I can't imagine anyone actually wanting to live with Mrs. Winch—can you?"

"Not easily."

"So now they've gone and we can relax." She gave a sigh of relief. "One more occasion on which I didn't shatter the image."

"What the children need now," Mrs. Mallin said, "is a good romp out of doors. But first let's get things back into order."

This, Edward found, meant retrieving toys from behind chairs and emptying the cupboards of all the miscellaneous articles that had been thrust into them. When everything was dealt with, he said that it was time he went back to the hotel.

"Thanks for the lunch," Estelle said.

"Thanks for the tea."

"Shall we see you again?"

"Of course. I'll come and say goodbye."

"Would you like me to drive you to Tom's?"

"No, thank you. It's a nice walk."

"Then . . . goodbye. For now," she said.

10

The business which had brought Edward up to Yorkshire on Tom's behalf was finished two days later. Tom expressed himself satisfied with the results, and Edward was free to return to London.

He paid a farewell visit to Pantiles. The fine weather had ended, and the children were playing in the room which had been allocated to him on his arrival. The house looked no tidier than when he had first seen it. Obviously Miss Curtis was not going to drop in.

Tom was not with him. He had business in York, and had dropped Edward at the house and promised to pick him up in an hour or so.

He had not seen Estelle since they had lunched, then taken tea together, but she had seldom been out of his thoughts. It was not a situation in which he had ever imagined he would find himself: attracted to a woman to whom his best friend could lay claim. It was reassuring to be going back to his own life, to scenes which would not recall those which had become so familiar.

When he reached the house, there was no sign of Mrs. Mallin or Mr. Mundy.

"They've gone to a nursery garden to buy some plants," Estelle told him. "They're thinking of turning the field into flowerbeds. They tried once before, about two years ago. Nothing came up but weeds, so they got discouraged, but Mrs. Winch seems to have started them off again. Have you really got to go back to London?"

"My job's waiting."

"Seems a pity, your leaving just as we'd got to like having you around. Tom will miss you."

"I doubt it. He's got plenty on hand to keep his mind occupied."

"Is the scaffolding down?"

"Yes. But that doesn't mean the job's done."

She was in the kitchen, ironing. A space had been cleared for the ironing board, and there was a pile of clothing in a basket on a chair beside her.

"Some jobs are never done. This one— ironing, for instance. Clothes—and food;

those are the two things you can't dodge if you're running a house. You've got to eat and you've got to dress. The rest—dusting and tidying and so on—can wait. I was very clever—I managed to make the ironing wait until the good weather changed for the worse. Is it still raining?"

"Yes."

"If it keeps on, I'll put the two boys into their macs and boots, and take them for a run by the river. Would you like me to make some coffee?"

"Why not let me make it while you finish the ironing," he surprised himself by saying.

He found what was necessary—cups and saucers, milk, coffee—and put water on to boil. The coffee was ready before the ironing was done; she switched off the iron and sat opposite him at the table. She sipped her coffee and then put down the cup and studied him for a few moments.

"We'll get news of you through Tom," she said, "but I'd like you to keep in touch. Have you thought any more about Tom's idea of your spending your holiday up here?"

"No."

This was untrue; he had given the matter a good deal of thought, and had decided that he had better go elsewhere—anywhere but here. This was Tom's territory. He discounted Brewster and van Leyden; he trusted Tom to hold his own against all competitors.

"You mean you've decided without even thinking about it?"

"I thought of going further afield."

"I know. Samarkand. Well, I think you're making a mistake."

"Why?"

"Because when you came here, you were stiff and formal. Now you're relaxed and unstiff and informal. That means we've done you good—us, or the air. So you ought to come back and spend some more time here." She went on without pause as her mother and grandfather came into the room. "I'm just telling Edward that he ought to spend his holidays with Tom."

It was not the first time she had used his name. More than anything that had passed, it gave him a feeling of belonging here.

Mrs. Mallin had taken off her mackintosh and held out a hand to take her father's. She threw both on the back of a chair and sat down wearily.

"I'm exhausted," she said. "So is your grandfather. We must have walked miles round that place."

"Well worth it," said her father, and turned

to address Edward. "Yes, why not?" he asked. "What better county than Yorkshire could you find for a vacation? Hills and dales, rivers and moors—and the sea."

"Tom invited him," Estelle said.

She was back at the ironing board. Mr. Mundy was seated; neither he nor Mrs. Mallin showed any disposition to move.

"Shall I make you some coffee?" Edward asked them.

"That would be nice," said Mrs. Mallin. "I like mine rather strong."

"Weak for me," requested Mr. Mundy. "We'd gone as far as talking about renting a house near the sea, but nothing came of it."

"Too much to pack," explained Mrs. Mallin. "You can't depend on the weather, so you need warm clothes for the children and light clothes and coats and macs and beach wear. It's more of a holiday to stay at home."

"And cheaper," said Estelle. "Mother, these rompers have shrunk. I shan't be able to get the boys into them."

"Are you sure?" Mrs. Mallin got up to look. "Yes, you're right. They're half the size they were. Never again will I buy that make. Oh— thank you," she said to Edward, as he put her cup and saucer on the table. "Just what I need."

"If you don't come here for your holiday," Mr. Mundy asked, "where will you go?"

"I rather thought of Majorca. Sailing."

"I envy you. I used to do a lot of that when I was young—sailing—but I'm past it now. Have you got a boat of your own?"

"Yes. I keep it at Newhaven. Tom and I have had a good many trips in her."

"The best holidays I ever had were in the Basque country. Peace and beauty. That was before they got trigger-happy." Mr. Mundy sighed. "So many parts of the world you used to be able to go to without fear of being kidnapped or shot at."

"And so many nice liners to take you to them," added Mrs. Mallin. "Now it's nothing but cruises. Not the same thing at all. I hear Tom's car."

A few moments later, Tom had joined them. Estelle left them to go and look at the children. Returning, she put the last ironed garment into the basket.

"I'm glad you took Edward to the Merlin," Tom said to her. "That was one of the things I haven't had time for while he's been here. Do you think we can induce him to come back?"

"We're doing our best. He says he's going sailing."

"Not if I can stop him," Tom said. "I've lined up my golf clubs and my tennis racquet and my squash racquet and I'm going to buy myself a couple of new sports shirts." He moved to relieve Estelle of the basket. "Where do you want this?"

"In the children's room. Thanks."

When he returned, Mr. Mundy asked him if he could spare a moment to look at the addition to the vegetable plot.

"If it isn't enough," he said, "you'll have to look elsewhere for vegetables. I won't be able to extend any more."

They went out together. Mrs. Mallin said goodbye to Edward and went to her room. Estelle and Edward were left alone.

"This is a goodbye visit, isn't it?" she asked.

"Let's call it a goodbye-for-now visit," he suggested.

She studied him for a few moments.

"I wonder whether we'll meet again—or not. I feel you're going for good."

"I'd like to say goodbye to the children," he said.

They went into the room he remembered so well. The baby had crawled under the bed. The two boys were attempting to put together a dismembered teddy bear. Estelle retrieved the baby while Edward took the bear and did a rough repair job that delighted its owners.

"If I stayed here long," he said, "I'd become a good handyman."

"Yes," she said. "I think you would. I can't imagine you ever adopting our fatalistic attitude to breakdowns. Will you let me know when you get those three pictures back?"

"Yes. Will you let me know when you decide to marry Tom?"

"Why are you so sure I will?"

"Because I think he's too good to leave for some other woman. He's special."

"I'll make a note." She led the way to the front door. "You came in the rain, you're going in rain. Don't forget us."

Their eyes met.

"I won't forget you," he said.

He left her and joined Tom. Soon they had driven away, the rain making a curtain to shut out the house that had come to mean so much to him.

His drive to London was made in continuing rain. The damp and the mist which had succeeded the spell of summer weather seemed to him to be a reflection of his own recent experiences. With an effort, he turned his mind to the work that would be awaiting him when he returned to his office.

He received a somewhat chilly reception from Miss Cave. She considered that he had stayed too long—longer than the business warranted, and vague suspicions had formed in her mind. Her professional interest in him stretched beyond the office confines and took in whatever she could learn of his leisure life. There had been one or two occasions on which she discovered that he had taken out a woman more frequently that his accustomed once-in-two-weeks, but the affairs had ended. Now she wondered whether he had become entangled up in Yorkshire, but the only calls he put in on his return were to Tom Parton.

He had not, he told Miss Cave, succeeded in seeing Mrs. Brockman.

"Her sister is living in the house," he explained. "Mrs. Brockman has gone, taking the pictures with her."

"Her sister must know where she is."

"If she does—and she says she doesn't—she would refuse to tell me."

"And no time limit? No hint of when she'll return?"

"None."

"You'll have trouble making the Brockmans believe that. They've been to the office twice while you were away. They're not prepared to wait until she feels like giving up the pictures. They feel you should find some way of making her part with them."

"If they'll find out where she is, and let me know, I'll take it from there. Do they know I'm back?"

"Yes. I told them I had no idea when to expect you, but they rang your rooms and found out when you were coming."

They called before the week was out. They had discarded any pretence of politeness, and told Edward frankly that they considered he had been outwitted.

"Bamboozled," Millicent snorted. "You've let her get away."

"You've mismanaged the entire thing," summed up Audrey. "You've wasted your time and our money."

There was a good deal more of this. Edward listened unmoved to the recriminations, but his dislike of the trio intensified, and he wished more than ever that they had taken their problem to some other lawyer.

Miss Cave showed them out at last, and he walked to the window of his room and gazed unseeingly at the view. Buildings, balconies, chimney pots, all too familiar to be noted; in his mind's eye was a house standing in a field, distant trees, a glimpse of a river, a

206

vegetable patch. Children seated on a rug in the sunshine, a young mother . . .

Depression swept over him. It was only too easy, he knew, to rationalise his situation. He had fallen in love. His best friend had a prior claim, and decency compelled him to stay out of the way. Here he was, keeping out of the way, and the loneliness and frustration he felt could best be countered by turning his mind to other matters. Other women. He had only to pick up a phone and dial. He had little vanity, but he knew that he pleased women who could see beyond his shy and formal manner. He had enjoyed their occasional companionship—lunches, dinners, rounds of golf and games of tennis. When companionship had drifted into an affair, he had taken what was offered with gratitude while it lasted, but with no undue regrets at its ending. Certainly he had never felt anything more than attraction. What he was feeling now was very different.

He could picture the life in the house in the north. She would wash up the children's breakfast things and ignore the rest. She would drive to the shops. She would make a meal for the children, and then she and her mother would have cheese and wholemeal bread and call it lunch. Old Mr. Mundy would eat tinned sardines and then, if it was fine and warm, would doze in a deck chair. There would be no haste, no bustle; there would only be peace, achieved in this case by ignoring or neglecting all tasks that were distasteful, and turning to the pleasant side of life.

He turned from the window to the telephone. With his engagement pad at hand, he filled his evenings. No more moping in his rooms. No more empty hours spent brooding. Work during the day, and amusement for the evenings.

To a limited extent, the treatment worked. He was kept busy in his office, and spent his leisure hours dining or going to the theatre or passing pleasant evenings in cosy flats inhabited by seductive hostesses. If he was not happy, he had the satisfaction of knowing that outwardly, at any rate, he appeared so.

To his surprise, he missed the presence of children. His was a world in which parents consigned their offspring to benevolent establishments which, for astronomical fees, took full charge and even, on request, kept the children during holiday periods. They occasionally came up to London for treats, and Edward met them and did his best to entertain them. But nobody, it seemed, had three babies to let loose to play in a field.

He was on his way to an early lunch one

day at the end of July, when he heard his name called. Halting, he found himself facing Anthony Brewster. He thought the warmth of his greeting must have surprised the other man.

"What are you doing in town?" he asked him.

"Adding to my stock-in-trade, I hope. Are you in a hurry?"

"No."

"Neither am I. I've got—" he consulted his watch, "forty minutes before meeting a tight-fisted old hag for lunch. How about a drink?"

"Good idea."

"Then follow me."

He led Edward to a side street in which was a small, Victorian building proclaiming itself to be the Golden Fleece.

"And well-named," Anthony said, as they carried their drinks to a table. "They fleece you, and you pay in gold." He sat on a cushioned bench in a window embrasure. "How're things with you?"

"Fair to middling," Edward answered. "Are you in London on business?'

"Yes, lucrative business, I thought—but that's not how it's turning out. I got a letter." He paused to drink. "I'm always getting letters from strangers offering me this or that rarity.

Old people, mostly, hit by inflation and selling off their treasures. What they treasure is very often not worth treasuring—but I took a chance this time and came to see the candlesticks this woman had described. They were good, but not as good as some I've got. I was wondering whether I'd buy or not, when I noticed—in a dark corner of a cabinet—a skillet."

"Skillet?"

"That's right. Cooking pot. A gem."

"A gem of a cooking pot?"

"Right. Silver. They're rare—very rare indeed in silver. You can't find many of them these days, but with luck, you may hit on one like this one I'm telling you about. Dates somewhere around the middle of the seventeenth century. About five or six inches in diameter. I was fool enough to put down the candlesticks and pick up the skillet and ask how much she wanted for it. That was my big mistake. We argued till we were tired, and then I suggested meeting for lunch today. So that's where I'm headed. She's all of eighty, lives in a kind of mansion-museum in Belgravia, and has a firm grasp on values."

"Why did she write to you? Surely she could have—"

"—found a buyer here in London. She could, but I'm getting known. Most of the people who write are merely using me as a valuer—as that woman did when she brought in three pictures—remember?"

"Yes."

"Well, all they want is to find out the value of the things they want to sell. But this was a genuine offer. Let's see what effect a good lunch has on her. Incidentally, did you see any more of . . . what was her name?"

"Mrs. Brockman." Edward signed to the barman to refill their glasses. "Have you been to Pantiles recently?"

"I was up there three days ago, trying to induce Estelle to come on this trip with me. No luck. Couldn't or wouldn't leave the children. How can a woman—a beautiful woman, an attractive woman—be happy leading a life like that? Because she *is* happy."

"I know."

"They're all happy—all three: the old man with his vegetables and his daughter with her picture frames. It's all right for those two; they've lived pretty full lives. But Estelle went straight into marriage and motherhood. I know those are considered in some quarters to be ends in themselves, but I also know there's a lot of Estelle that isn't being used. Did you know she could sing?"

"Yes."

"She played the violin until she married, since when she's never touched it. Her grandfather was first violinist in a York orchestra. Then when Estelle's husband died, he moved into her house with his daughter, and they concentrated on picture frames and cabbages. Drink up. I've time for one more. Going abroad this year?"

"I don't know. I can't make up my mind."

"I'm tied to the shop. There's no one I can leave in sole charge for more than a few days. Still, if I'm not away, I can keep an eye on that van Leyden, who's always taking his blasted horses round to Estelle. He's in love with her, and if you want the truth, so am I. I don't regard him as a potential threat—he's too full of himself to impress her. Tom's another matter—but if she wanted him, what has she been waiting for? Is that the time? God, I'll have to hurry. Nice to have run into you. Bye."

He was gone—handsome, upstanding, intelligent—and in love. But there was hope for him. He was living within a few miles of Pantiles, he was an old friend—though not as old as Tom. He had a thriving business and, Edward judged, a good deal of money.

He lunched alone. The restaurant was almost full, but he managed to get a table to himself. His encounter with Anthony Brewster had left in his mind a picture of Pantiles, and he had a heart-shaking longing to go up on some pretext and instal himself at the Cross Keys.

She had refused to come to London with Brewster. That was something. She was at home, safe with her children. While he was far away, and missing her sorely.

The matter of his holiday became one of urgency. Miss Cave wanted to know where he was going, and when, and for how long.

"I can't make arrangements for the staff," she said severely, "until I know what your plans are. This should have been settled in March."

"I'll think it over tonight," he said, "and let you know in the morning."

The morning brought, not decision, but Tom. He came to London on an early train and telephoned Edward's office before midday.

"What's brought you up to town?" Edward enquired.

"Wedding. A cousin several times removed.

She's forty-two and it's not so much a wedding as a celebration. That'll occupy my afternoon, but I'm free for lunch."

"And dinner?"

"No. I'm going back north as soon as I've got out of my wedding garments. Let's meet for lunch at your usual place. Make it early."

"I'll be in the bar at twelve thirty."

"Good. Incidentally, have you made any firm holiday dates yet?"

"No. Today was to be the deadline. My secretary's not pleased."

"Hold everything until you've heard what I've got to say."

Over drinks, he put his proposition briefly.

"I've got to take time off," he said. "I've been driving myself into the ground ever since that fire. I can't take more than a week." He leaned forward to put down his glass. "You remember that cottage I own up on the moors?"

"Yes."

"James Weaver—remember Jas?"

"Yes."

"Well, he and his wife Frances are staying in it, but they want company. They want me— and you. She's pregnant and can't join him in striding over the countryside as she used to. She's promised to relieve us of all chores if

214

we join them. So how about it? You and I like them both, and we haven't met for years. They're good value all round, and there'd be a bridge four for the evenings. Take it or leave it."

Edward spoke unhesitatingly.

"I'll take it."

It solved all his problems, he thought with relief. He would be near York and could perhaps see Mrs. Brockman. He would be able to visit Pantiles, but he would be based at the cottage. He liked both James Weaver and his wife. The situation of the cottage was one of isolated beauty. There was a river to fish in, and rabbits to shoot. The sea was almost at the door. And Miss Cave would be delighted that he had finally reached a decision.

He brought his attention back to Tom, who was talking.

"—their first baby. They'd almost given up hope. After all, they've been married—how long?—eight years."

"Nine."

"That's right. Nine. God, time flies, doesn't it?"

"Yes. Is he still in the insurance brokers' business?"

"And prospering. She came into some

money when her father died. They used it to buy their house in Hampshire."

A waiter brought menus, and they studied them in silence for a time. Their meals chosen, they sat back to await the refilling of their glasses.

"Dates," said Tom. "Can you get away as early as next Friday?"

"Yes."

"Then let's fix that. They won't be at the cottage much longer, otherwise you could have stayed when I left. But I hope you'll come back to the hotel for a couple of weeks. I won't be able to spend much time with you, but it'll be nice to have you around."

"I'll do that. Thanks."

"Incidentally, all at Pantiles sent their love. Old Mundy nearly came to the wedding—he's the bride's godfather—but he wouldn't go to the trouble and expense of hiring an outfit. His own—he found when he looked—was like a sieve. Moths or mice. He's given them a nice wedding present—a pair of antique tankards Tony Brewster sold him. I'm giving them a whisky decanter—pretty useless, as they're more or less teetotal—but nice to put on display."

They parted after lunch, and Edward rang for Miss Cave and informed her that he would be away for three weeks beginning on Friday.

"Up in Yorkshire," he ended.

"Aren't you going to Majorca? You talked about going. And you mentioned sailing."

"Perhaps next year," he said. "I'll come in on Friday morning for a couple of hours."

But before Friday came, he had a visit from Mrs. Brockman. Miss Cave, lips tight with disapproval, ushered her into Edward's room and shut the door with a snap.

"Surprised to see me?" she asked.

"Yes. Have you come to tell me you're giving up the pictures?"

"No. Not yet. Not for a while yet. I've made a date in my mind—October tenth. That's the day I first went to that house for an interview. Are they all three chewing their moustaches in rage?"

"They're angry, yes. You realise that you've put me into a very difficult position?"

"It's not your fault, is it?"

She was wearing a dark green tweed suit and a round green felt hat. She looked neat, but unseasonable.

"If you want to know," she continued, "I'm not finding it so easy carting those pictures about. I can't just leave them in a hotel room, can I?"

"I hope you won't."

"So where I go, they go. I nearly took them back to my own house, but I knew that if they were there, some nosy parker would find out. And my sister's no use at lying, so she'd let on they were there. Any news of up north? I know you've seen Mr. Parton. I was going to go to that restaurant for lunch to talk to you, like I did before. But I saw you and him come in together, so I went and had a bite at the place on the corner. I suppose he's here for the big wedding? I know the bride. She used to visit a house I was working in up in Doncaster. Lot of money, but no looks. I'm glad she found a taker at last."

"Are you staying in London?"

"No—I told you. I'm staying in Yorkshire. But I had to come and tell you about the date I'm letting the pictures go. October tenth. Where will you be then? On holiday, I suppose."

"No, I'll be back in London. I shall be away for three weeks—starting the day after tomorrow."

"Where'll you be?"

"Like you, in Yorkshire. At first in a cottage on the moors, and then at the Cross Keys."

"Did Mr. Parton tell you it's doing even better than it did before the fire? When he did the repairs, he added one or two

218

improvements. I was there one day last week, looking."

Studying her, he thought that she was getting less enjoyment than she had anticipated in holding up the return of the pictures. What had seemed fair revenge had now turned sour. She admitted as much when she rose to take her leave.

"I'll be glad to be back in my own house," she told him. "My sister's no use in the garden, and mine's going to ruin. You'd think she'd at least do a bit of weeding, wouldn't you? It'll soon look like a field—like that field at Pantiles. Any news of them?"

"Not very much."

"I think about them a lot. I keep wondering when they'll get round to giving the house a good tidy-up. I'd go and help them if they asked me. Well, goodbye for now. Maybe we'll run into each other some time while you're on holiday."

He saw her go and experienced a moment of compassion. She had made herself homeless and saddled herself with three large works of art. Well, it was her own doing.

In his rooms, packing for his journey north, he experienced for the first time a feeling of being hemmed in. The space which had once

219

seemed so adequate now appeared to him to have the dimensions of a rabbit hutch.

He went to the window. There, flowing past, was the river. Seen not between green banks but between grey buildings. He longed, suddenly, to be away from man-made structures; to be out in the open, walking on dusty lanes or on overgrown grass. Suddenly, he was glad to be going; happy without reservations. He would be in beautiful moorland—and she would not be far away.

11

James Weaver's nickname—Jas—dated from his schooldays. He was now thirty-four and had been married for nine years. He had been for a brief spell at the same school as Edward and Tom, but had changed it for a less demanding institution. Left in infancy without parents, he had been brought up by a series of elderly relatives, none of whom had been able to understand or control his exuberance. Passed from home to home, he had lost none of his capacity for enjoying life to the full. There was, Edward had always thought, a resilience in his constitution that resisted all Fate's attempts to subdue him. Though intelligent, he had never in his life succeeded in passing an examination. Careers opened before him, and closed when it became obvious to his employers that he considered the complexities of business an enormous joke. Nature had made him happy, and he continued happy and made a great many of his fellow men happy.

Nobody took him seriously, but there was beneath his ebullience, his verbal extravagances, something essentially good, a kind of innocence, that prevented people from underrating him. His wife, a calm, sensible woman of thirty, regarded him as a child who must be given his head—and protected. She managed the generous income she had inherited; left to him, it would have melted in the warmth of his willingness to help friends out of financial difficulties.

He was a tall man—Edward's height—but of lean and lanky build. Nobody except his wife had ever considered him handsome.

He greeted Tom and Edward, on their arrival at the cottage, with pleasure that seemed a continuation of their last meeting.

"Greetings, brothers! Come in, come in and make yourselves at home. Let me look at you. Sunburned Tom and paleface Edward. Poor paleface, cribbed, cabined and confined in lousy London. Come and look at Fran. Behold her—great with child. My child. After years of strenuous endeavour. I shall never know what we did wrong before we got the hang of it."

Fran's greeting sounded like strings after brass.

"Wonderful of you to lend us this cottage, Tom."

"Why do the English call cottages cottages that aren't cottages?" Jas demanded. "This is no cottage. It's a house of stone, commodious and comfortable. Or perhaps not so comfortable. Whoever built it forgot one or two essentials like running water and North Sea gas and switch-on electricity. Nice big windows. I bet the moorland air blows through them in winter. Shall I show you to your rooms?"

"No. You can unpack that basket," said Tom. "It's got drink in it."

"May God bless you," Jas said fervently. "I got in as much as the local store stocked, but it was a mere half dozen bottles. Fran and I were praying for your arrival. What did you bring, Edward?"

"Tom sent me a list. I've brought all the items that were on it."

"Tins of ham, I trust."

"Yes. And pears and apples and two pineapples and Spanish olives and French cheese and Indian chutney."

"Come with me," Fran said. "You can unpack it, I'll put it away."

"Who's doing the cooking?" he asked as they went to the stable-sized kitchen.

"Jas. He's good—don't you remember?"

"I remember. No plain food. Solely luxury items. How do we get milk and bread and so on in this expanse of nothing but Nature?"

"We go and fetch everything. It's only five miles to the shops."

"What else is at the end of the five miles?"

"What Tom calls the village. They sell enough to keep body and soul together. If we run out of nourishment, someone'll have to go into Whitby and stock up. How do you think Jas is looking?"

"Very well. So are you."

"I'm enjoying myself. Another four months and there'll be a little Jas. Jas junior. What kind of father do you think he'll make?"

"Kind."

She was small and sturdy. Seeing husband and wife together, Edward thought they made a picture of a restless dog tied to a post—free to leap and bark ceaselessly, but kept within a limited circumference. She was amused by Jas, but her amusement had a plainly protective edge.

There was no domestic help to be had at the cottage. The four inmates divided the work between them and settled down to enjoy their holiday.

It became obvious at once that shooting rabbits was not to be expected of Jas. While attempting to fire at rabbits, he was several times on the point of puncturing Tom or Edward. He was relieved of his weapon, and shooting for the pot was abandoned. It fell to Edward to drive to Whitby to buy whatever was needed in the way of meat or fish.

He returned one morning to find a familiar car parked at the gate. To his amazement, Estelle was walking towards the cottage. She was carrying the baby—Tom, beside her, was leading Hugo; Jas was in charge of Maurice.

Tom was looking pleased with himself.

"I pinned Estelle down to a day's visit," he told Edward. "She promised—and here she is."

She was more sunburnt than she had been when Edward had left for London. All three children were brown, all three full of energy and curiosity to see what was to be seen. The men delivered the visitors to Fran, and she led them indoors for milk and biscuits.

It was a happy day. So successful was it, in fact, that Fran was moved to beg for another visit.

"I second that," declared Jas. "These three

are far and away the most picturesque infants I've ever had the pleasure of meeting, and I'd like Fran to see as much of them as possible while she's in the process of putting together a baby of her own—and mine. Why," he asked Estelle, "don't you go and bring some luggage and join us?"

Tom was swift to urge this plan on Estelle.

"There's room and to spare," he told her. "There's a big room—let's call it the nursery— which opens straight on to the moors. Please, Estelle! Do come. It'll do the children a lot of good—this air's wonderful."

"Like the wine," averred Jas. "They'll drink it in and thrive."

Estelle stood looking at them. It could be seen that she considered the plan an agreeable one. But she hesitated, and began to point out certain drawbacks.

"The children make a lot of work."

"We're used to work," Jas told her. "We work all the time. At least, the others work and I keep them up to scratch. I'm the foreman, the overseer, the boss. If only you'll do us the honour of joining us, I'll see to it that you're relieved of all responsibility for your three beautiful babies. Fran will take over."

Happily, Fran concurred. "I'd love it more

than anything. And it would be good practice for me."

Estelle, unable to resist the genuine warmth of the invitation, said that she would love to come. Tom drove her back to Pantiles in his car, and they returned with luggage and some equipment for the children. The weather, which since June had shown a tendency to showers, now became dry and almost too warm.

A new pattern of life was soon established. Estelle and Fran stayed with the children, for the most part out of doors. Jas, deprived of his gun, took to sketching. Tom and Edward went for long walks. And when Edward drove to Whitby, he was now accompanied by Estelle.

"You can leave the babies to Tom and me," Fran told her.

Tom chose baby-minding rather than shopping. Edward and Estelle set off together.

"I don't feel right," she told him. "I keep reaching for the children. Isn't this a wonderful holiday? Why do you and Tom have to leave?"

"He's got the hotel to run. I think, in a way, he's anxious to get back to it."

"He's never worried about it before. Do you think he ought to put in a manager?"

"I can't see him handing over to anybody."

"Neither can I. Have you made any progress with that picture business?"

"No."

"Have you seen any more of . . . what's her name? Mrs. Brockman."

"Yes. The whole business is absurd—childish. But I think she's had it in mind for a long time. That's to say, I think she made up her mind that she'd keep the pictures when her husband died. I wish some other firm was dealing with her."

"So do I, since she annoys you so much. Have you ever seen a pair quite like Fran and Jas?"

"Never. But she knew him a long time before she married him. She knew pretty well what she was getting. Did you know I met Anthony Brewster in London?"

"Yes. He likes you. He says that behind that impassive mask there's a nice chap. His own words." She paused. "I never saw the impassive mask. That night when you came in on a flash of lightning, the mask had slipped. You just looked like an orphan of the storm. Wet hair, wet face, wet mackintosh. And we took you in—in more senses than one, because you didn't get your money's worth."

"Don't be too sure about that."

"Well, you got a miserable breakfast. And no coffee. Which reminds me—have you got the shopping list?"

"No. You took it from Tom and put it on the table."

"And left it there. How good is your memory?"

"Baby food, milk, bacon, meat, marmalade, eggs . . ."

They became a familiar sight in the shops they went to. It was taken for granted that they were living together; the baby food clinched the matter. If the list was a short one, they put the purchases into the car and walked down to the sea. He loved to see her keeping pace with him, lithe and graceful. He could put away, on these mornings together, all thoughts of a future to be lived without her.

But those mornings were not to end. Tom, himself obliged to return to work, refused resolutely to take Edward with him.

"There's not the slightest need for you to come," he told him. "I'll be too busy to entertain you."

"Our arrangement was that—"

"I know what we arranged. But I'd like you to stay on. The two girls will spend their time with the children, and Jas'll be out of it. You'll balance the party."

"I came to Yorkshire to see something of you," Edward said.

"And you'll come again to Yorkshire to see me. But I'm asking you now to stay on here and keep an eye on all my guests."

Edward said no more. He was to stay. Tom had decreed it. There would be more mornings spent driving over the moors to Whitby.

Tom went away, and the bright mornings continued, and so did the shopping. Edward and Estelle went in his car, waved off by Jas and Fran and the three children, who seemed completely happy to be left to Fran's motherly ministrations. They all went, on warm mornings, to bathe in the sea, plunging in and coming out shivering. Estelle invariably left the shopping list behind. She and Edward talked of the past and the present, but made no mention of the future. The afternoons were spent on the moor, the babies became an all-over brown. And Damien, walking with more and more confidence, sometimes walked into trouble.

"It was like this," Jas explained. "He likes to clutch at things as he goes staggering round a room. When he hung on to the table, fine, but when there was a tablecloth on it and he grabbed that, all the king's horses and all

230

the king's men couldn't put the crockery together again."

"Was he frightened?" Estelle wanted to
know.

"Frightened? He was enchanted. He wanted me to put back the things so's he could do
a repeat performance. What worries me is
who's going to pay for the breakages. Me,
because I was on father duty at the time—
or you, because he's your child? If he were
older you could deduct it from his pocket
money."

"Replacing those plates should be easy,"
Fran remarked. "Everything in this so-called
cottage was bought by someone who didn't
believe in making things match."

Edward took his turn at watching the children. He found it a less demanding task than
he had anticipated.

"They're a happy lot," he observed to Estelle. "They don't quarrel."

"That's because I taught them how to be
friends."

They were driving home from the shops—a
long way round, to take in more ground than
they had hitherto covered. The views were
magnificent; every curve of the moorland road
brought fresh beauties. The skies were clear,
the breeze cool.

"This," she said out of a comfortable silence, "is the nicest holiday I've ever had."

"Wrong tense. You're still having it."

"But not for much longer. You'll go away in one direction, and Fran and Jas will go in another, and I'll go back to Pantiles and get on with real life."

"Isn't this real?"

She hesitated.

"No," she said at last. "It's something I imagined. Or perhaps—yes, it's real. Real companionship. Have you had much real companionship—like this?"

"No."

"Nor have I. Mother, grandfather—nice to have around, but . . . well, this is different. How many women have you taken out since you stayed at Pantiles?"

"Do you want a rough figure?"

"No. One by one. First?"

"I took a girl called Barbara to the theatre."

"And then what? Home?"

"She has a studio apartment in Bayswater."

"I see. Next?"

"I took a French girl called Lisette to dinner in Soho."

"She sounds like one of those La Bohèmes. Does she own a studio apartment?"

"No. She was staying with friends."

"Bad luck. Next?"

"I went to some parties."

"Escorting anyone?"

"Yes. I can't remember quite—"

"That's what I think you are—one of those men who doesn't remember quite. I wish I knew whether these mornings are going to be something you won't remember quite."

"These mornings," he began—and broke off.

"Don't stop. Or do. Stop the car and tell me."

He stopped the car and switched off the engine. Then he turned to study her, and spoke.

"Why do you ask questions when you already know the answers?"

"To hear you talking. I like to hear you talking. You don't talk all that much. And I want to fill in a background—your background. You're pretty cagey—do you know that? You don't *tell*. There's a lot more of your life than just coming into Whitby shopping with me. I'd like to know about it."

"You know all there is to know. Office, some exercise—and some diversion, with men or women. And that's all."

"And to that you now have to add three children and a muddle-minded mother."

"There's nothing muddled about your mind."

"Oh yes, there is. That's why I'm trying to keep you separate. Apart."

"I don't want to be separate. I'd like to fit in somewhere."

"You've already fitted in—but this is just an interlude, isn't it?"

He could not answer. Suddenly Tom came into his mind—Tom, who had left them and gone back to work. He had all but forgotten Tom.

"Well, isn't it?" she asked again.

"No. To me at least, no."

"Thank you. That makes me feel better."

There was silence. But his arms were reaching out to draw her to him—and she was making no resistance. She lay against him, quiet, unmoving, and then she raised her head and he put his lips on hers.

He could not count the time that passed before he released her. Freed, she took a deep, tremulous breath.

"That," she said slowly, "makes me feel better still. It's like the answer to a question that I didn't ask."

He did not reply. He switched on the engine; the car took them back to the cottage, to the children, to Jas and Fran.

They prepared a picnic and ate it on the bank of a stream. Fran and Jas elected to stay at home with the baby. Edward, watching the two boys pretending to fish, had a suggestion to make.

"I'd like to buy them a dog," he said.

She shook her head.

"No. Animals are out."

"A large breed of dog," he went on, unheeding. "A big, gentle dog. Protective, but lovable."

"No."

"The sort of dog they can put their arms round. A dog to play with."

"No."

"Any other objections?"

"Heaps. My husband pointed out all the drawbacks. Licking the children's faces. Biting bits off biscuits that the children are eating. Tripping them up when they're running. Picking up their toys in his mouth. You can't call that hygienic, can you?"

"No. All the same, I'd like to choose a nice faithful companion for them. We could drive to those kennels near Whitby and choose one together."

"No."

Nevertheless, that afternoon found them at the kennels, the two boys, enchanted, dividing their attention between a beautiful golden labrador puppy and a floppy-eared spaniel. It was a close finish, but the labrador won. Estelle, wearing a resigned air, watched as a collar was fitted, feeding and drinking bowls chosen, food and feeding instructions carried away. The puppy, already aware of being attached to a happy home, sat at the back of the car with the boys and panted expectantly.

"So now we're all supplied," Estelle said. "The boys have got a pet, I've got a problem— and you've got your own way. Nothing like persistence. You should've bought a bulldog."

Edward said nothing. One of his reasons for buying the puppy—now named Paddy— was only now becoming clear to him. He wanted to leave with them something of his own, something that, when he had gone away, would be a reminder of the time he had been with them.

"Say thank you to the kind gentleman," Estelle instructed.

They put their arms round his neck and pressed their faces against his.

"Nice gentleman," said Hugo.

"Nice Paddy," said Maurice.

He kept his mind on his driving and tried to ignore the feeling of satisfaction that the contact with their soft little arms had given him. Estelle watched him curiously.

"I suppose you feel one of the family now?" she asked.

"More or less."

"Tom will be annoyed. He's been trying to foist a dog on us for ages. So has Brian van Leyden."

The names, falling into the quiet contentment of the afternoon, gave him a feeling of coldness. Yes, there was Tom, and there was van Leyden and Anthony Brewster. He would have to go; they would remain—close to her, able to see her, to speak to her.

"I wish," she said suddenly, "that you lived nearer."

"I'm only a few hours' drive away."

"And at the end of the drive, a different world."

Yes, he acknowledged to himself. A different world. Office, and rooms that he had come to think of as cramped, and unsatisfying contacts with a series of acquaintances.

"Do you want to go back?" he heard her ask.

He took his time, rounding a curve with care and stopping at the junction with the main road.

"Wanting, or not wanting, doesn't enter

into it," he said. "It's my life—I have to go back to it."

"And this was just a sort of interlude?"

"A very happy one."

"But you think it would have been happier if Tom had been around all the time?"

It would have been safer, he thought despairingly. It would have been a constant reminder of how matters really stood. It would have been a brake.

"Tom," he said slowly, "is my oldest friend."

"I know. You keep saying so, even when you don't actually say it."

Once again, he had no reply. The puppy, perhaps remembering who had paid for his transition to this satisfying new life, was licking the back of his neck. The boys were doubled up with amusement. He stopped the car and mopped his neck.

"*I'll* buy *you* a dog," she said. "To remind you of us."

"I won't need reminding. And I couldn't keep a dog in my rooms."

"Then move out of them." She swung round to face him and spoke with a kind of suppressed anger. "Move out of them. Move into a big house with a garden. Have a dog— several dogs. Have cats—or a horse. Have a wife and six children. Get out of your snug little hidey-hole and . . . and *expand*. And stop accepting what you think you can't change. Stop accepting situations. You changed my mind about letting the children have a dog—didn't you?"

"Yes, but—"

"Tom's an old friend, but you don't owe him anything. You needn't let him shape your life. Stop being so . . . so *controlled*."

"Controls are necessary. If this car didn't have controls—"

"—it would take off on its own and explore new territory." She leaned forward and placed a brief, soft kiss on his cheek. "New territory." She turned to face the road. "Sorry about that," she said in a different tone. "It's the puppy's fault. It's catching, all that kissing. Hadn't we better head for home?"

He put the car into gear. They got to the cottage and showed Jas and Fran the new acquisition.

"Just what's needed," Jas said approvingly. "He'll play with them and protect them. He'll keep them well exercised. It makes me want to go out and buy a dog of my own."

"Wait till our baby's walking," Fran advised. She looked across the spreading moorland. "Hasn't it been wonderful here? How lovely it would be to have my baby here."

"Not lovely at all," Jas said. "No amenities. No running water, no anything that you'll need when the time come. No telephone."

"How did women manage here in the old days?" Fran demanded.

"I'm not interested in the old days," Jas said. "These are the new days and I'm going to see to it that you get the benefit of the new methods of bringing children into the world."

"There's only one method of bringing children into the world," Estelle told him. "Leave it to Fran. She'll manage without any new methods."

"And in the meantime," Fran said, "may Tom be blessed for his bounty. Let's phone tomorrow from the village and ask him to try and come out for a day before Edward leaves."

It was the first mention they had made of his leaving. Edward found himself wondering whether the references to Tom were made with the intention of keeping him in their minds. He decided that they were. Fran and Jas were not fools, and they were not blind. There was not much to see in the relations between himself and Estelle—but they would see whatever there was.

He decided, then and there, that he must leave. He must get away. It was not too late, but it would be too late if he delayed his departure. He had fallen in love—so much was irrevocable—but he did not care to guess how much, if anything, Estelle felt for him. She was warm and friendly, but she was warm and friendly by nature. She liked him, but that was perhaps all.

He offered to do the telephoning in the morning. Leaving Estelle to complete the shopping list, he got through to the Cross Keys and spoke to Tom.

"There's a general feeling that you ought to come back for a day or two," he told him. "How about it?"

"Impossible. I'm up to my eyebrows. Are things going well?"

"Things are going very well. It's been a perfect holiday. But look, Tom—"

"Well?"

"I'm afraid I'll have to cut it short."

"Why?"

"There are a couple of things I must look into at the office."

"Can't they wait?"

"They could, but they're on my mind. I'd like to get back."

There was a pause.

"If that's the way you want it—" began Tom.

"Not *want* it. But I must get back."

"Then you must. It's been nice seeing you. Will you look in here on your way south?"

"I think not."

"Then let's make a date for Christmas."

"Christmas'll be fine."

He rang off. He did not mention the conversation until he and Estelle were facing Fran and Jas across the breakfast table, with the children close by and the puppy at their feet. Then he told them that he would be leaving that afternoon.

"Why?" Fran asked, as Tom had asked.

"Pressure of business." It was Estelle who answered in an expressionless voice. "Men must work, and women must weep—isn't that how the song goes? Are you," she asked Edward, "going to look in on Tom on your way home?"

"No. I think we made a date for Christmas."

"We'll all look forward to seeing you," she said evenly.

He packed, helped the others to set out a salad meal, and after sharing it, carried his suitcase to his car. It was not an intimate farewell. Fran kissed him, Jas gave him a hearty pat on the shoulder, the children put their arms round him, the baby waved. And Estelle had little to say.

"Been nice having you."

"Thank you. I'm sorry I'm going."

"So am I. Take care of yourself."

He was gone. He was driving away, driving back to an existence which now seemed bleak in the extreme.

He passed within a few miles of the Cross Keys, but his pace did not slacken. There was nothing he felt he could say to Tom.

12

He did not go back to his office until the weekend was over. He passed the intervening days in walking, playing golf or tennis and dining alone at restaurants to which he had not been before. He did his best to keep his mind from the cottage he had left so precipitately; only when he looked out of his window and saw the river flowing past did he find it impossible not to imagine himself back at Pantiles.

Miss Cave gave him a cool welcome and ran through the details of the work that had been done while he had been away.

"You're going to have trouble with the Brockmans," she ended. "They've got tired of waiting passively for those pictures. They want action."

"They're at liberty to take any action they please. But first, they've got to catch their hare."

"It's a pity you agreed to act for them."

"A great pity."

"I'm beginning to feel sorry for them."

"The more I see of them the more I feel that they're only getting what they deserve," he countered with feeling.

She permitted herself a slight lift of the eyebrows. He did not often speak with so much force. Going back to her room, she decided that his holiday could not have been a success. She wondered if there was a woman in the case—but his telephone calls revealed that although he was seeing three or four women, he was certainly not singling out any one of them in particular.

Two weeks after his return, he entered his usual restaurant for lunch. Across the room, in the chair that Mrs. Brockman had once occupied, he saw Estelle. He had to stop and draw a deep breath before he could complete his journey to the table.

"Sit down," she invited, and waved a hand to indicate the chair opposite. "Make yourself at home."

He sat down. She was wearing a linen suit, the buttons of which were an imperfect match. She was hatless, her hair, sun-bleached, falling loose on her shoulders.

"A great surprise," he managed to say.

"To you and to me, both. I made up my mind—as you did—all in a moment. I said to myself: 'I'll go and have a day in London.' It wouldn't have been possible if Jas and Fran hadn't volunteered to take over the children for the day."

"Are they well?"

"Dog and all. But it hasn't been the same since you left. I always know what Jas and Fran are thinking; they tell me all the time. I miss trying to read behind the façade, as I have to do when you're around. Have you got those pictures back yet?"

"No."

"Mrs. I-always-forget-her-name Brockman was on the same train as I was."

"Did you speak to her?"

"Only when we met at the taxi stand."

"She came from York?"

"Yes. With only one small canvas bag. No room in it for pictures. You haven't lost any of your tan."

"Nor have you. Did you come to London to shop?"

"No. I came to see you. It's that old situation over again: if Mohammed runs away from the mountain, the mountain has to go in pursuit. What are we going to eat?"

"I'd like a light lunch."

"So would I, especially after a hot train journey. Can I have Vichyssoise and then asparagus and then cold salmon with lots of salad?"

"Surely." He gave the order.

"Make that for two," he said.

"And strawberry ice cream."

"Cheese for me," he told the waiter.

He ordered white wine, and she watched him smell and taste it before nodding to the wine waiter.

"Nice," she said, sipping it. "Why haven't you asked me why I came all this way to see you?"

"I haven't had time. Why did you?"

She answered with simple directness.

"To find out why you ran away."

There was a long pause. She sat with her eyes on him, waiting patiently for him to speak.

"I left the cottage," he said at last, "because I decided that it was time I came back to London."

"You decided very suddenly." She broke a bread roll and buttered it. "To tell you the truth, it was Paddy who made me decide to come to London. He went round making mournful sounds in all the places you'd frequented—it made one's heart heavy to watch him—and then he asked me outright to find

247

out where and why you'd gone. So I said I'd find out. So here I am, not finding out."

"How did you know about the lunch table?"

"Easy. When Mrs. Brockman and I were waiting at the taxi stand, she told me she'd once made a descent on you. She was in a communicative mood—but she didn't mention pictures. What message shall I take back to Paddy?"

"Tell him not to disturb the status quo."

"You think his Latin will be up to it?"

"Yes." His voice changed. "That goes for you too, Estelle. Please."

"What exactly is the status quo?"

"Tom loves you. I love you. But Tom comes first."

She spoke after a pause.

"I doubt if I can make Paddy understand that. He doesn't think Tom's as important as you do."

"Ask him if he had a bone and another dog came up and tried to take it from him, what he'd do."

"He'd fight. So would the other dog. And it's the other dog we're discussing. You said you loved me. What happens if I say I love you?"

"You don't. You can't. Tom's an old and trusted friend. I'm a . . . a newcomer, someone who—"

"—who touched down for a time, and then took off. Isn't that cowardly?"

"Yes. It's cowardly—but it's right. How could we ever be happy if we betrayed Tom?"

Neither he nor she had done justice to the excellent food. Plate after plate had been carried away barely touched. Now she was toying with her ice cream. She was pale but composed.

"That wraps up everything," she said. "I can go home and tell Paddy about the status quo." She put down her spoon, abandoned the ice cream and looked round for her handbag. "From here," she said, "I'm going north. Are you sure you won't change your mind and come with me?"

"Quite sure." He made a low sound of despair. "Oh Estelle—"

But she had pushed back her chair and was rising. It was over. He had done what he felt he had to do. Who could tell when he would see her again?

The weeks that followed were the most miserable he had ever spent. He worked mechanically; he took exercise without pleasure. His friends found him preoccupied.

Then one morning the telephone rang at

his office, and he heard the first sound of a voice from Yorkshire.

"Edward? Tom. This is a pretty dud line—can you hear me?"

"Yes."

"Then listen carefully. I haven't much time. There's to be a kind of dog show up here. Not a serious affair—just fun. It was Estelle's idea. Proceeds to go to famine relief. I wasn't over enthusiastic, but once we'd put the word round, the thing seemed to take fire. Burgeoned. We'd put the entrance fee as high as possible—thirty quid per dog. That way, I thought we'd soak the rich and rake in a couple of thousand. But we've got seventy-eight entries already, and they're still coming, partly due to the county-wide advertising campaign that's being managed by Brian van Leyden. Pamphlets, posters, house to house leaflets. He's paying for it all. We've got some good prizes. We—are you still there?"

"Yes."

"Tony Brewster gave us a couple of good vases, and the tradespeople are coming up with generous handouts. Why I'm ringing you now is to ask you to come up and be one of the judges."

"Judges? My God, Tom, I don't know the first thing about—"

"—about points. That's just the point, excuse the pun. I've explained that this is fun. No nonsense about points. You merely pick out the animal you like best, and hand it its trophy. It's to be the smallest or the biggest, the longest or the shortest—that kind of thing."

"But—"

"We've roped in seven judges. You're the eighth. Mr. Edward Netherford of London. You shouldn't have any difficulty about getting up here—we've fixed it for a Saturday, so you'll be free. Thanks a lot."

"But I haven't—"

"I ran into your Mrs. Brockman in York, and roped her in as a judge. She's worth her considerable weight in gold. She's undertaken to get the barn ready."

"Is that—?"

"—where it's to be held? Yes. Looks good on the posters—'historic fifteenth-century barn'."

"Historic?"

"Yes. Wars of the Roses. Can't stop to go into details. I'll send you a pamphlet with the dates and so on. Thanks again."

The line went dead. Miss Cave came in to tell him that the three Brockmans were waiting to see him, and he received them looking, he hoped, like a judge.

The interview was brief, and not pleasant.

"We have come," Audrey began without preamble, "to tell you that we have decided to take the matter of the pictures out of your hands."

"Because," Millicent explained, "we consider that you have done nothing towards their recovery."

"Nothing whatsoever," said her sister.

"Damn all," said her brother.

"Moreover,"—this was Millicent at her most magisterial—"we are all agreed that your attitude towards this matter has left a lot to be desired. You have seemed to us almost uninterested in getting these pictures back."

"Mrs. Brockman left home," Edward reminded them firmly, "taking the pictures with her. All I could give you was her assurance that she would eventually return them. She has fixed in her own mind a limit to the time she will go on with this rather childish charade."

"And you believed her. But we don't," said Audrey in a tone of finality." We haven't the slightest hope that she won't keep the pictures until something is done to find her and apply some kind of force to make her give them up."

"And as you appear unable to do this, we are going to approach another firm of lawyers," said Millicent. "I would thank you for your help if you had given any. Good day to you."

Her brother and sister made no polite farewells. Edward rang a bell on his desk, they were shown out and Miss Cave came back to ask what had taken place.

"Gone for ever," he told her, and paused to savour a dream-sequence in which Mrs. Brockman, defiant and obstinate, was tailed by a series of detectives in trilby hats and dark glasses.

"I suppose you're glad to see the last of them," Miss Cave observed, "but the trouble is that they'll talk."

"Smirch the reputation of this firm? I doubt if anybody would take them seriously."

"Do we send them a bill?"

"No. They wouldn't pay it."

She left him, and he returned to work on the affairs of more congenial clients. But in his mail was a flimsy paper on which was printed the time and place of the forthcoming dog show. It was an advertisement which Edward thought had a certain appeal. It was headed 'Dog's Day,' and carried a sketch of the barn in which the show was to be held. All dogs, of whatever breed, size and temperament were cordially invited. There would be a panel of eight judges. Dog food and refreshments would be on sale. The entry fee per dog was thirty pounds.

"Is that a misprint?" Miss Cave asked, gazing at the paper with an astonished expression.

"No. The fee was fixed when they thought they wouldn't have many entries. Now they've got almost a barnful, and the thing is still escalating."

"Famine relief. How much do you think they'll make?"

"Thousands. They're a generous lot, those northerners, when they're sure they're getting something for their money. This time, they're getting some fun. I'm one of the judges."

She opened her mouth to give an incredulous exclamation, but managed to substitute something more polite.

"I didn't know you were an expert in—"

"This is only a matter of choosing the dogs I like best. I daresay a large proportion of the entrants will be mongrels."

"It's on a Saturday. Perhaps I'll go. What's the entry fee for non-exhibitors?"

"Five pounds."

"Five—!"

"Famine relief."

"Is this going to be one of those affairs that eat up the takings in vast expenses, leaving a mere pittance for the poor and needy?"

"If I'm not mistaken," Edward answered, "there won't be any expenses. The barn belongs to Mr. Parton. The publicity is being donated by one of his friends. The refreshments will be given gratis by the catering firm or firms. If you're thinking of going, I could give you a lift up there, but I may be staying the weekend, so I couldn't bring you back."

"Thank you, I'll find my own way up. And not alone." Her lips set in a firm line. "I'm going to make a party of this. There are a lot of people in this firm who can afford to spend five pounds on feeding the hungry."

The office total reached fifteen. Miss Cave, for once neglecting her work, spent much of her time during the next week arranging for a bus to take the party up to York.

"Coming back on Sunday night," she told Edward. "It's a good opportunity to get in some sight-seeing."

Edward was not much interested in the rising enthusiasm for the expedition. His own mind had seized and clung to one fact: he would be seeing Estelle. Everything else was subsidiary. He would see her. She would be there and so, doubtless, would be her mother and her grandfather and her children. And the dog. Paddy, of impeccable pedigree, would surely appear at future, more prestigious shows, but he would make his début on Saturday.

"Did you say," Miss Cave asked him, "that Mrs. Brockman was to be a judge?"

"Yes."

"As you're no longer representing her stepchildren, I suppose you consider it unnecessary to inform them that she'll be there?"

"Totally unnecessary."

Miss Cave gave a satisfied nod.

"I thought that's what you'd say," she said, allowing herself the merest trace of a satisfied smile.

He left London early on Saturday, on a morning that presaged a perfect day. By midday he was skirting York. Soon the Cross Keys was in sight, unfamiliar by reason of the scores of people milling round the building and the barn.

He saw at once that Mrs. Brockman and her helpers had done wonders in transforming the barn from a vast, bare structure into a series of neat booths, soon to be occupied by the entries, which had reached a final total of one hundred and twenty.

"And we were turning them away at the end," Tom, appearing from the hotel, informed him. "Would you have thought that

256

an idea, a half-serious idea of Estelle's, could turn out like this? The Lord Mayor's going to put in an appearance. So are all the county bigwigs. So are all the littlewigs—the butcher and baker and so on."

He was in high spirits. Edward wondered, with a pang, whether Estelle had at last agreed to marry him. The success of this undertaking must have made him feel elated, but there was something in his air that seemed to be a quieter, deeper satisfaction.

Anthony Brewster was superintending the arrival of the food and drink. So unexpectedly large had been the flood of entries that two large marquees had been erected for drinks and refreshments. Brian van Leyden was placing numbered cards in the booths that the dogs would occupy. A contingent of the hotel's employees, clad in cool and casual clothes, were busy giving help where help was needed. The sun, sensing that too much heat would be unwelcome, came and went. A mild breeze fluttered the flaps of the marquees.

"If you're doing nothing, you can help me to get these tables in position," Anthony called to Edward. He wiped a sweating brow. "Whose idea was this? Lugging heavy loads about on a tropical afternoon. Look and see whether the tea urns have arrived, will you?"

They had arrived. Innumerable bottles of orange or lemon squash had arrived. Rows of tea cups stood on one trestle table, regiments of glasses on another. Water was being piped into the barn, to fill the receptacles the dog owners would bring with them. More and more people—assistants—were arriving. There was no sign as yet of any of the Pantiles party.

Lunch was the same for everybody—mountains of ham or cheese sandwiches provided by Tom, beer or soft drinks, hot or chilled coffee. Brian, a sandwich in each hand, came over to join Edward and Anthony.

"I've been doing some rough calculations," he said. He was biting into each sandwich alternately. "I reckon this canine circus ought to net more than seven thousand, as near as makes no matter. Where's it going to? Oxfam? Or is it going to be spread around?"

"No idea," said Anthony. "I've just been looking at the prizes."

"So have I. A goodly array," said Brian. "I liked that ornamental dog bowl you contributed—among other things. I wouldn't have said that two policemen were enough to stand guard. Isn't it time Estelle got here?"

"She's doing what the rest of the exhibitors are doing," Anthony guessed. "Keeping their dogs away until starting time. That Mrs. Brockman made a good job of the booths, didn't she?"

Edward moved away to join her. She was holding out a large mug to be refilled with tea.

"I couldn't have managed without all those workmen," she said in answer to Edward's congratulations. "They told me I'd have made a good sergeant-major. How are the Brockmans getting on?"

"I don't know."

"They're your clients, aren't they?"

"Not any more."

"You mean you gave them up?"

"The boot was on the other foot."

"They sacked you?"

"You could put it that way, yes."

She gazed at him, took a sip of tea, and spoke.

"I suppose you blame me."

"No. I blame myself. For agreeing to work for them."

"That's what I told myself just after I took on the job of housekeeping for them. I only stayed for Mr. Brockman's sake."

"Where are the pictures?"

"In a safe place, like I told you. Once I got them stowed safely, I could enjoy myself. It's been like a nice little holiday."

He had lost interest in the conversation. Through the newly erected entrance gates he could see Estelle. She was pushing the pram with the three children in it and the puppy frolicking behind. Her mother and her grandfather walked on either side of it. Tom ushered them past the two gatekeepers and led them towards the barn. They were at once joined by Brian van Leyden and Anthony Brewster. Edward, who had moved forward, stopped and watched them go. At the entrance to the barn, Estelle looked round, saw him and waved.

She looked, he noted bitterly, happy and carefree. The cloud that had rested over their last meeting had obviously been dispelled. She was at home, among friends, close to her children—and that appeared to be as much as she needed. Tom was beside her. They went into the barn and out of sight, and he turned to find Mrs. Brockman watching him intently. She spoke in a dry tone.

"She's got three after her. What would she do with a fourth?" she asked. "All of them with money and to spare. All of them living the good life. Why don't you join them?"

He did not reply. He left her and walked slowly to see the play park that had been arranged for small children. There were low swings, miniature slides and some accident-proof roundabouts. There were already a number of children in the enclosure, mothers on guard.

The crowds were arriving. Guides conducted exhibitors to their booths. In the distance, a band began to play.

"The York Junior Brass band," a voice said behind him. "Giving their services for free."

He turned. Estelle looked up at him and laughed.

"You've strayed," she told him. "You're supposed to be in the barn, taking a preliminary look at the entrants. Wait till you put yourself in there—it's like Bedlam. Come and see."

It was noisy, but it was not disorderly. The variety of dogs exceeded anything he could have imagined. To the spaniels and terriers he recognised, were added exotic breeds with coats like feathers; pocket-sized, ratlike creatures and towering, dignified, lionlike, king-size animals. The thought of having to judge them seriously and not, as was now the case, for amusement, made him turn pale.

Mr. Mundy was pushing the pram, with Mrs. Mallin beside him.

"Going to the children's enclosure," he called above the din.

Tom was in the booth, guarding Paddy. He motioned Edward towards the judge's stand. Here Edward found Brian and Anthony and some people he did not know.

"We're judges, too," Anthony told him. "And this—" he indicated a large woman wearing an elaborate summer dress and several rows of beads, "is Lady Venson. Allow me to introduce Mr. Edward Netherford. Commander Rhodes—General Lasker. Lord and Lady Strannock will soon be—oh, here they come. That makes us complete."

Estelle had taken over charge of Paddy. Tom was free to go round the grounds, seeing that all was going well.

The judging proved popular. The prize winners were an appealing black and white mongrel (longest tail), a quarrelsome dachshund (shortest legs), four dogs whose breeds were unknown to Edward (most pointed nose, longest coat, largest ears, loudest bark) and—chosen by General Lasker—Paddy, for having the most appealing expression. Consolation prizes went to a collection of restless mongrels. Tom went to the stand and, cheered loudly, gave out the awards. Then the owners were invited to tea in the hotel, and the judges were led by Tom to have tea or drinks in his private rooms.

It was past eight o'clock when the grounds began to empty. The children's park had long been deserted. Tea had given way to beer. The cake stand was empty, the ice cream finished, innumerable packets of potato chips eaten and their containers littering the ground. Bottles of wine were being raffled.

When the last of his guests had gone, Tom put a hand on Edward's arm.

"We've got to talk," he said. "The question is where? I don't want any interruptions."

The only quiet and unoccupied place they found was the bridge room. Here Tom pulled out two chairs, sat on one and waved Edward to the other.

"Take a seat," he invited. "This won't take long."

"First of all, congratulations."

"On what?"

"A highly successful show. Have you any idea what the total intake will be?"

"Something in the seven thousand bracket. That's not what I want to talk about. The subject is you. Yourself."

"Go ahead."

Tom leaned forward.

"You're aware, of course, that I'm in love with Estelle?"

The unexpectedness of this opening made

Edward stiffen. He took a moment or two to recover.

"Yes," he said. "I know that."

"And van Leyden and Brewster are in love with her too—you also know that."

"Yes, but—"

"Don't interrupt. Any moment that door might open and some straggler or other will appear. Let me proceed. You, yourself, are in love with Estelle. Right?"

There was a pause.

"How did you—" began Edward.

"You told her and she told me. She went to London to see you. You sent her back to me."

"I give you my word—"

"That's irrelevant. Let me outline the position. You fell in love and then took a Little Lord Fauntleroy stance—I was first comer. Et cetera. So you kept your mouth shut and bolted back to London."

"All I—"

"—and bolted back to London. Without so much as reminding yourself that Estelle could have had me years ago, but chose to be a sister instead. Tony and Brian were always non-starters. If they had been—if she'd looked like taking one of them—I'd have fought, because I knew I could make her a better husband.

But when it came to you, things were different." He paused momentarily. "You see, I know you pretty well. I knew you were in love with Estelle almost as soon as you knew it yourself. I felt sorry for you. You wouldn't have time, I thought, to make an impression. But you did. Then I was sorry for myself. And still am—but it's my turn to act Little Lord Fauntleroy—or do I mean Sydney Carton? You love her and she loves you and that's enough for me."

Edward stared at him, tried to speak but succeeded only after a third attempt.

"Look, Tom—"

"Let's check. You love her?"

"My God, yes. But—"

"I have her word for it that she loves you. She thought that going to see you in London would get some kind of response out of you, but you pushed aside your fruit salad, ignored all the implications and said: 'Go to Tom—he loves you and I, his best friend, cannot betray him.' You always had a sentimental streak but I thought years of hobnobbing with me would have knocked it out of you. Let me conclude by saying that there is nobody else— nobody in this world—I would have stepped aside for. There's not much nobility in it—she doesn't want me." He pushed back his chair.

265

"Now I'm going to find her and I'll tell her I've done your proposing for you and I'll send her in here to give you her answer. Stay where you are, and don't move. And good luck."

The door opened and closed. He had gone.

13

"Perhaps it's asking too much of you," Estelle said.

"It's only a simple matter of a move, isn't it?" Edward asked.

They were in his car, halfway between York and London, speeding south. Tom, the children, Pantiles were left behind. Before them was the necessity of finding a house in or near London.

"It's a matter of moving all our earthly possessions. Do you think we'll find what we're looking for?" she asked.

"In time, yes. Or we might be lucky and hit on something more or less straightaway. If not, you'll have to go back to the children, but you'll have to come to London again to look at any possibilities I manage to line up."

"We're not looking for anything impossible," she pointed out. "Just a house."

He smiled. "Just a house. Six bedrooms, six or perhaps a dozen bathrooms, balconies facing south—"

"I've changed my mind about the balconies. Children climb up and fall over. You don't need balconies if you've got a nice big garden."

"Does it have to be so large? There's Hyde Park and Green Park and Kensington Gardens—isn't that space enough?

"You have to take the children there and watch over them. If you've got a nice garden, you put them out there and just glance out of a window every now and then. You won't forget a lovely big playroom on the ground floor, opening on to the garden? And a big kitchen."

"Have you considered how you're going to heat the nice big playroom and the nice big kitchen?"

"All houses of the kind we're looking for will have central heating. Old-fashioned, perhaps, but better than nothing. Do you want a small study, or a sort of combined study-library?"

"I shall build myself a retreat at the far end of the nice big garden," he told her.

It was her turn to smile. "You're scared, aren't you?" she asked him. "You're staring into a future filled with the noise of children.

You visualise an existence in which you lose your identity and drown in domesticity. Right?"

"Only too right. As I see it, there's no escape."

"As *you* see it. Where did you say we were going to stop for lunch?"

"Not yet. About forty more miles."

"Then I've got time to explain about domesticity. Ready?"

"Yes."

"Domesticity is making a home. There's no point in making a home and not spending time in it. Domesticity is a way of life that's made up of healthy, happy children, good meals, a sensible routine—and dotted with occasional sorties to meet friends. Not acquaintances—friends. Or to dine out."

"You've left out the business end."

"The office?"

"The office. Adam delved while Eve span."

"I haven't left out the office. I wake you at seven. I give you a cup of tea. You bound out of bed and do your pull-ups. You have your bath, shave and don your City suit. You come downstairs to a table in the corner of the kitchen. You can smell coffee. You can see hot rolls, butter and marmalade—or honey, if you prefer it."

"Where are the children?"

"They had their breakfast while you were in your bath. They are now in the garden or the playroom, according to weather, and are waiting to say goodbye. You drive away. You return to find drinks ready in the drawing room, the children in night attire, dinner sizzling in the oven. You play with the children and help me to bed them down. We return to the dining room, to a table laid with pretty mats and lit by candles. We eat soup, some light fish and perhaps, as a treat for you, some two-minute steak. We put the plates into the dishwasher and carry our coffee into the drawing room. You tell me how your day went at the office. We study the engagement book to see what we've got next week in the way of entertaining or being entertained. We find to our relief that we're only committed on one evening. We go to bed. So what do you think of that picture of domesticity? How does it sound to you?"

"Improbable."

"Improbable?"

"And out of date."

"Out of date?"

"Yes."

"What's out of date about a nice home life?"

"It was all right in Queen Victoria's time. But that cocoon existence has gone."

"Only because a lot of women decided that they'd be happier taking a letter, Miss Brown. The cocoon—the enclosed life—is still there for anybody who wants it."

"But nobody does any more. Mothers want to go on living the good life. You're the exception."

"I've just told you what I consider the good life."

"I know. But wait and see if it works."

"Why shouldn't it?"

"Because I know something—not much, but something about you," he said. "You will wreck the washing machine and the dishwasher and fail to find anyone to mend them. You will apply your theories about not letting the housework become a burden. The children will dominate the scene. Nothing will sizzle in the oven because you forgot to buy the things that sizzle. I shall end by doing a full day's work at the office, and going home to be butler-cook-houseman. I don't see anything to laugh at."

"You'll have to change your viewpoint again. If nothing sizzles, if there isn't much dinner, you'll keep your nice slim outline. Don't you believe that I'll keep our home beautiful?"

"No. Perhaps I'll get used to it. You've left out the animals."

"There's only Paddy."

"There'll be more. There'll be white rabbits in hutches, white mice in cages, hamsters in houses, several cats and all Paddy's descendants. We'd better fix on a house close to a riding school—that'll take care of the ponies. Do we have to have hanging plants? They're tricky obstacles for a man my height."

"Don't you like them?"

"No."

"All right. No hanging plants."

"Thank you," he said taking her hand. "Do you like the look of this place for lunch?"

"Yes."

"Good. Then we'll eat."

Over the menu, she raised the question of finance.

"Can you afford to do all we're planning to do?"

"With luck. I'm not poor. I'll only be poor when we've got through a year or two of what you outlined as domesticity. I've made out a list of my assets—you can look through it at your leisure. It's not complicated. To it you can add two probable legacies—a godfather and a great-aunt. Have you decided what you're going to do with Pantiles?"

"Yes. I'm going to do what I said I'd do—leave my mother and grandfather in it. They wouldn't like to have to face turning out—and what would they do about the picture frames and the vegetables?"

"Will you charge them a token rent, as I suggested?"

"Yes. Something very small."

"Can they afford to live on what they've got, plus what the picture frames and the vegetables bring in?"

"Yes."

"Then you've nothing to worry about. Neither have they. So why are you looking so pensive?"

"I'm just beginning to realise what a sea-change this is going to be for both of us. From poky rooms to a big house, from country to city."

"From order to chaos."

"From peace to—"

"—domesticity. Have you begun to miss the children yet?"

"No. I've said I'll stay three days. I'd like to get back before that. But I suppose we can't find a house in three days, can we?"

"We might. I'm banking on the fact that we're in the market for the kind of house most couples wouldn't look at."

She was eating with obvious pleasure.

"When I'm happy, I'm hungry," she explained. "Who looks after your rooms while you're away?"

"The porter keeps an eye on things. Incidentally, I didn't tell him I was coming back so soon."

"Will you be able to get in?"

"Yes."

But when he opened his front door and ushered her in, he was struck yet again by the cramped appearance of the accommodation. Was it here, in these box-like rooms, that he had lived for so long?

She had paused in the living room.

"Small," she commented.

"Yes."

It must look very poky indeed to her, he thought, coming as she did from the freedom and spaciousness of her home.

"Come and look at the river," he said.

But the river seemed brown and sluggish, and the buildings bordering it had a grim, industrial look. She did not linger at the window.

"What I don't understand," she said, "is how you can fit everything you own in the world into these rooms."

"I can't. I don't. Every set of rooms has a large box room on the ground floor."

"What's in your box room?"

"Spare suitcases, a trunk or two, surfboard, skis, skiing boots, that kind of thing."

"Can we look?"

"Of course."

They went down in the lift and he inserted his key into the box room door and opened it. She stepped inside.

"Tidy," she said.

"That's the porter's job, to keep it tidy. I don't come down here unless I need to, which isn't often."

"I've never been on skis and I've never been on a surfboard."

"You'll soon learn. We'll take the children skiing."

"So young?"

"Scandinavian children are born on skis."

She sighed happily.

"I can't wait to see Hugo and Maurice whizzing down a mountainside," she told him. "Dressed in those lovely colourful outfits." She nodded to some large packages stacked against the far wall. "What's in those?"

He was looking at them with a frown.

"They're not mine," he said in a puzzled voice. "The porter must have put them in here by mistake. They—"

He stopped. An idea, one he immediately

thought absurd, had entered his mind. Large, square packages, well wrapped in thick brown paper. Three. One, two, three.

He strode across the room, lifted one away from the wall and stood gazing at it.

"It can't be," he said.

She came to join him.

"What is it?" she asked.

"I don't know. At least, I think I do know. But how in God's name . . . Ah!"

"Ah what?" she enquired in mystification.

He did not answer. He was carefully stripping off the wrappings. She watched him with interest.

"A picture," she said as the last layer of paper was removed. "A picture—but not yours?"

"Not mine, no."

"It wouldn't be one of those pictures you've been trying to—"

"She told me, but I didn't think it was important—she told me that one of her relations worked here."

"The porter put them here?"

"She and the porter, both. She told me they were in a safe place."

"So they are."

He was re-wrapping the picture.

"She knew I was up in Yorkshire. She took

a chance—and it was a good chance that I wouldn't come down to this room before she decided to give up the pictures."

"So now what? You tell her you've found them?"

"I do not. Can you carry one of them? I can take the other two."

They carried the packages out to the lift. Edward went back to lock the door of the box room. Together they took the pictures up to his rooms.

"Now what?" she asked. "You leave them here?"

"No. The porter would see them. I'm going to take them to the office. When she comes to fetch them, they won't be where she left them."

"But she'll know you've got them. Why don't you give them back to the owners?"

"That would be letting her off too easily. I shall tell her I don't know where they are—which will be true, as I'll tell my secretary to find a place for them. Mrs. Brockman will, I hope, pass a week or so worrying. After which I shall tell the owners I've got the pictures, and will present my bill. When it's paid, I shall let them have the pictures. Do you see anything wrong in that plan?"

She came over to him and put her arms round him.

"Nothing at all wrong," she said. "But I've always been on Mrs. Brockman's side."

"So have I. But justice is justice."

"You're so right," she said admiringly. "Kiss me."

14

A house in London. It was, the house agent informed them cheerfully, a good time for buyers. They should have no difficulty in finding what they wanted. But this optimism did not outlast his realisation that Estelle wanted several contradictory features. It was to be a large house, but easy to work. A garden, of course, with trees and a spreading lawn, but nothing that would need a gardener. It must be an old house, but not so old as to be without modern conveniences. There must be several bathrooms. And naturally, there must be a view of the river. The house should be in a quiet neighbourhood, but there must be shops not too far away. And schools. And a park for the children to play in and meet the neighbouring children.

The house agent struggled on, but the weeks went by and brought nothing that was acceptable. Estelle came south by train whenever inspections were to be made, but had to make the journey so many times in vain that the agent began to grow morose.

"You can't always get exactly what you're after," he told her. "You have to settle for the nearest to what you want."

"But it's *somewhere*, the house we're looking for," Estelle pointed out. "I'm not being fussy. All I want is a nice place that's been lived in by people who like space and comfort. You wouldn't expect me to put three babies into one of the awful high-rise boxes, would you?"

"I'm doing my best for you," he reminded her.

"I know you are, and we're very grateful."

At last a compromise was reached. They found a house, which though somewhat decayed, had most of the amenities Estelle had insisted on. There was a good view of the Thames from the front windows. There was no park, but there was a pleasant garden surrounding the house, and a small public one near by. The neighbourhood was not quiet, but there were schools and there were shops. When money had been spent on a face-lift, when modern heating had been installed, they would have almost all they wanted.

"Except bathrooms," Estelle said. "Imagine

only two bathrooms for all those bedrooms. Didn't you tell us the house had been used as a boarding house?" she asked the agent.

"Yes. But not for long," he said. "It's going to cost you a lot to fix it up the way you want it."

"I daresay, but it's going to be permanent. Once we get in, we stay in. And when it's ready, it'll be a lovely house."

Miss Cave, to Edward's irritation, emerged as an expert in matters relating to building. She looked through the estimates, haggled over price and paid frequent visits to the house when the alterations were put in hand. She produced a stalwart nephew who undertook to put the garden in order. She went shopping with Estelle—who had not asked her—and advised on covers and curtains. She went hunting for antiques in the dim recesses of second-hand furniture shops and sent Edward to see what she had found.

"Why doesn't she attend to her office work?" Estelle asked.

"She *is* attending to it," Edward assured her.

"Then how can she fit in all she's doing outside the office?"

"She did the same for my father when he furnished his cottage in Somerset. Unasked."

"I see. You're going to say she does it out of kindness, and not because she's got an interfering nature. Aren't you?"

"Yes. You'd better get used to her. She's one of the strings attached to marriage with me. Have you made up your mind yet about that woman who came and offered to work three days a week?"

"Yes. No good. She said that children made work."

"Well, they do, don't they? I've heard you say so."

"Perhaps—but I didn't like the way she said it."

"That's the third woman you've turned down."

"Fourth."

"It's not a small house. You might find yourself—"

"—without anybody. I'll risk it until I get someone I can work with."

"The difficulty will be to find someone who'll work with *you*. You're not the world's tidiest housewife."

"That's one of the strings attached to marriage with me." She paused. "That's something I worry about."

"Marriage with me?"

"Trying to live up to your bachelor standards.

Have you really thought about that?" She reached up and put her arms round his neck. "Have you visualised coming home in the evening to find things in a muddle?"

"There's a saying about taking the rough with the smooth." He stroked her cheek gently. "Lovely skin you've got."

She released him and spoke soberly.

"My big problem," she said, "will be learning to—"

"You needn't go on. You're going to say that you'll find it hard to treat me as a father. But I've made my own plans for taking second place—or should I say fourth place, after Hugo and Maurice and Damien? You'll find that all three of them will soon make their own adjustment. They'll accept me as a father, after which you take your place as a mere mother and I become the head of the household. So you can put your mind at rest on that score, and start thinking about household help."

There was help at hand. Mrs. Brockman telephoned to Edward at his office and informed him that she would be joining him at lunch the next day.

She was at the table when he arrived, dressed exactly as she had been on her first appearance in the restaurant. She greeted

283

him without ceremony and said that she would like a tomato juice.

"Not full of ice," she warned the waiter. "I like it just as it comes. People talk about chilling this or that," she went on to Edward, "but all it means is that they freeze all the taste out of it. How are Estelle and the children?"

"Haven't you ever dropped in to see them at Pantiles?"

"I haven't been in Yorkshire for a while. Not since you gave those pictures back."

"I sent the family a bill."

"They paid it?"

"They did."

He was waiting for her to order.

"All I want, on a muggy day like this," she said, "is something light."

"Fish?"

"No, not fish. A nice omelette made with good, ripe tomatoes, with a green salad—none of those tired outer leaves, just a nice heart."

Edward ordered fish for himself. When the wine waiter appeared, Mrs. Brockman asked him if he could produce a glass of cider.

"Certainly, Madam."

"Not too cold, mind."

"No, Madam."

"And not too acid." She turned to Edward.

"I'm going to enjoy my food," she told him, "and then I'm going to do what I came to do—put a proposition to you. But eat up your fish first."

Her conversation could not be called general. It centred on Mr. Mundy and Mrs. Mallin, and then went to Estelle.

"A nice girl you've got," she told Edward. "She's got her faults—who hasn't?—but she'll make a good wife once she gets the hang of what's required of her. She won't waste your money—she's been used to managing on a small budget. It's a pity her husband threw away so much money fixing up that house of theirs. He didn't leave her much, from what I can make out. The old man, Mundy, only has enough for himself, and there'll be less when he gets too old to work that vegetable patch. Mrs. Mallin does well enough with her picture framing—you won't have her on your hands."

Edward ate, and listened, and marvelled at the knowledge of the family that she had picked up in so short a time. But he knew that any information she sought, she would not hesitate to ask for.

He found her good company. He was sorry when he had to make preparations to leave.

"Hold on." Mrs. Brockman drained her

glass of cider. "There's this proposition I've come to talk about. I'll put it to you straight, the way I always like to put things. You ready to hear it?"

"Yes."

"Well, it's this: I want to work as housekeeper to you and your wife, when she becomes your wife. I want . . . No, don't say anything yet. Let me finish. I'm a good housekeeper. I'm a good worker. And I need work. I'm sick of doing nothing. Oh, I know I go in for all that committee stuff, and I try to do good where it's needed—but I want a steady job. A proper, regular job. I know I've got a nice home, but there's not enough to do in it to keep me happy. I want a fixed job with a fixed salary. A daily routine. I can work for you because I like you both and I like those three children. I've talked to my sister. It was really her that started this idea in my mind. She wants to leave Durham and come and live in York, and she's agreeable to selling up her house and coming to live in mine. We get on well together—and if I'm in a job, she'll be happy on her own. I'll go up there for my holidays. She's got lots of friends in York; she'll be all right." She leaned back in her chair. "And that's it. Except that I'd need a woman to help me with the rough."

There was silence for a time. Then Edward spoke.

"It seems to me that there's a lot more in this for us than there is for you," he said.

"That's what wages are for—to make up the difference. I'd expect to be well paid, and for that, I'd work well. And though it's not for me to say, you need me."

"Yes," Edward admitted. "We need you."

"And what's most important of all, I like those three kids." She waved aside the waiter's offer of coffee. "No thanks, not for me. Well, Mr. Nethercliff, what d'you say?"

"We could try it."

"Good." She made preparations for departure. "I'm going back to York on the 4.10, and I'll pay a call at Pantiles and tell them what we've fixed up."

He felt he ought to say something about consulting Estelle first, but he decided that Mrs. Brockman was able to take care of all minor details.

"What you have to do now," she told him, "is put household chores out of your mind and get on with your own job." She rose. "And if I haven't said it before, I'll say it now—it'll be a pleasure to work for you."

Returning to his office, he knew that a weight had been lifted off his mind. Something told him that this arrangement would be a success. He did not think that Mrs. Brockman had decided to undertake a full-time job with them before making certain it was what she wanted. She had doubtless debated the matter before putting it to him. She would run the house and she would share the children with Estelle. She was sturdy and cheerful and sensible.

And in time, perhaps, he thought, she would learn to address him by his correct name.